THE CREW

The Crew

MICHAEL PATRICK COLLINS

UPFRONT PUBLISHING
LEICESTERSHIRE

The Crew
Copyright © Michael Patrick Collins 2004

ISBN 1-84426-291-X

First published 2004 by
UPFRONT PUBLISHING LTD
Leicestershire

Printed by CopyTECH (UK) Ltd.

Prologue

The torrential rain of the night eased and finally stopped, the only sound now that of water slowly dripping from the roof. It was the low growl of the dog that disturbed him, then the yelp as the machete struck home. In the hour before dawn, fully awake and shivering with fear, he lay waiting, listening. The opening rounds pierced the door in the ground floor room where he slept. Splintered wood and the heavy bullets from an old .303 rifle filled the air. All passed over him until inevitably one, deflected by the rusty iron hinge, smashed into his left leg tearing its way upwards through muscle and flesh, finally coming to rest in his groin. Too terrified to cry out, he bit his lip as the blood flowed.

The noise shifted. Now they were pouring rifle and automatic fire into the floor of the house above their heads for, like all the houses, it was on stilts. Here his father, mother and baby sister slept. Voices, whispers, now heard openly, betrayed the local dialect; he knew there was nothing he could do. For what seemed ages, the firing continued and then quite suddenly he heard something else; the raiders left. He could not move at first. Finally, pulling a splinter from his arm, a cry of pain escaped, followed by seconds of terror - had they heard?

Moving slowly, he climbed the stairs, blood flowing down his leg and arm to form slippery pools on the wood. Fearful of what he knew he would see, he entered the bedroom. A spasm of retching began.

The initial shots had blown large pieces of floorboard through the bodies. His father and mother had died instantly, the exit wounds all too clear in the early morning light. Little Shari had survived until the machete had been used. The stink of blood emptied his stomach and he collapsed.

As dawn broke he knew he had to move, had to get away.

The raid had been well organized; seven houses hit, all killed it seemed. This one was Negroes against Indian, next week would be the opposite. The Intelligence Corps officer stood tight lipped, looking at the mutilated bodies. Bastards don't deserve to live. Why are we always too late? Usual crap, I suppose, interviews with the head man, excuses, incriminating evidence slipped into the river for the piranha.

Helicopters were landing now with suspects collected for interrogation, although he doubted he would find anything. These people were stoic about these things, until their private 'payback time', of course.

'Charlie 2' was the Alouette helicopter of the Army Air Corps, tasked with the deep patrol. The plan had been to seal the river above and below the village, with troops landed from the Royal Air Force Whirlwinds, while Charlie 1 and Charlie 3 patrolled each side for any escaping terrorists. Charlie 2 was the back stop, about five miles west, patrolling the line between the rice paddy and the jungle.

The infantry captain saw him first, nudging the pilot and pointing to the levy at the boundary of the rice. The division could not have been clearer, golden rice moving gently in the humid wind to the east, then the dead straight brown line of the bank with the lush green of the swamp on the western side.

At 3,000ft you could see everything here. A lone figure limped slowly towards the mill a couple of miles away. They watched for a few minutes as he stopped, hearing the aircraft, then running in a crablike way. Silly, really, thought the pilot, cautious, though. These bastards had a few automatic weapons that looked to be the new AK47s, the 'I' Corps man had said.

Positioning behind at 500ft and slightly to one side, the infantry captain trained his Stirling sub-machine gun on the runner and waited. It was obvious that the man was wounded, whoever he was.

The collapse was not long in coming. A quick circuit of the surrounding area cleared it of ambush. The pilot slowly came to a hover over the levy, gently lowering the chopper to the ground, its tail hanging out over the stinking swamp.

They waited as the aircraft shut down. The faint clicking of the cooling engine was soon the only sound. There was no movement from the man as they slowly approached on either side of the thin track that divided the rice paddy from the swamps of the inland; their guns were trained on the body.

He lay there barely conscious, aware of the gathering flies at his thigh and the quiet as the helicopter engine was shut down, knowing that this was the end.

'Looks as though he's Indian,' said the pilot. 'Well, the I Corps guy said it was Negroes on Indians this time.' 'Jesus! Look at that leg. My guess is he's a runner, maybe one of the victims.'

The pilot yelled back to the chopper where the observer waited. 'Bring the first aid kit, Harry.' Not that it would do much for this poor bastard – the kits they carried on the choppers were next to useless.

It took about ten minutes to use every dressing the kit had and slow, but not completely stop, the bleeding.

'I think that I had better take this bloke back to Atkinson. I'll call Charlie 3 in to pick you up, unless you want to come with me?'

The infantry officer declined. 'No, call Charlie 3. I had better get back and report this to 'I' Corps man; he will want to speak to this one, if he survives. Who is Charlie 3 today?'

'Deano, good bloke,' muttered the pilot, 'he'll look after you.'

'Harry, we are going to take chummy here to Atkinson? Mr Grey is going to stay and wait for Charlie 3.'

Moving back to the Alouette, the pilot eased himself into the seat and cranked up the tactical radio. 'Charlie 3, Charlie 2?

A brief pause and Deano's Lancashire twang broke through the dull hiss of VHF radio static. 'Charlie 3, go ahead.'

'Charlie 2, we've got a casualty about two miles southeast of the Burma rice mill, on the levy between the rice and the swamp. I've got a guy from the Buffs with me, wants you to pick him up. I'm going back to Atkinson with the body. It's going to be touch and go for the casualty so can you collect?'

'Charlie 3, sure, with you in ten. Give him a flare just in case.'

'Charlie 2, Roger that.'

The boy, for that's all he was, was loaded into the left-hand stretcher and strapped in. Hope the poor kid doesn't wake on the way, thought the pilot. Still, looking at the bloody mess on his flying suit, he thought he would be lucky to wake at all.

The infantry captain waved as they lifted off, a lonely figure on the dyke.

Now on the air traffic radio, the pilot called in, 'Atkinson Charlie 2' 'Atkinson Charlie 2.' Silence. 'Damn! Too bloody far.'

'Charlie 2, this is Clipper 549, you wanna relay?' The slow drawl from the daily Pan Am to Miami just airborne came through the headset.

'Yeah, 549, Charlie 2 is a military helicopter on casevac. Can you relay to Atkinson? Charlie 2 is inbound, ETA 45 minutes, severe casualty on board, gunshot wound to the leg, requires medico at the field.'

'Roger that, Charlie 2 standby.'

The pilot listened as the American 707 relayed the message.

'Charlie 2, Clipper 549, all okay, buddy, hope it all works out for you.'

'Thanks, Charlie 2.'

It took all of 45 minutes to get back. The doctor stood by the Land Rover, which was his makeshift ambulance. As he landed, the medics rushed over and with Harry the crewman, they eased the young Indian boy out.

Speaking briefly to the pilot, the doctor jumped into the Land Rover and disappeared, the dust slowly settling as the vehicle turned the corner.

The pilot looked at the crewman and himself and, without a word, both walked down the track to the showers. The chopper, too, would need a wash. The best part of eight pints went a long way, he thought. Wonder what the poor bastard's name was.

The I Corps man had told them that the boy was the sole survivor from the seven houses that were targeted. Twenty three people, including eight children that night. He should really go and see him, the Doc reckoned his chances were better now. Even so, he would always have a limp.

Doc had said that the boy hadn't said a word. Maybe a friendly face might help and God knows he had no one now. Bit like me, thought the pilot.

The hospital was little more than another hut, with the usual smell of antiseptic and medicine added.

Doc met him. 'Still hasn't said anything. All we know is that his family was one of those butchered. We think his name is Kassim – one of the villagers reckons it's him. I guess he saw it all. As near as I can tell, he would be about 14.'

They approached the bed, the boy's leg supported and swathed in bandages. His eyes moved to focus and a slow awareness, recognition.

Georgetown, Guyana, 2001

Odd to think that I had been here over 30-odd years ago. It hadn't changed much in that time, just another ex colonial backwater mouldering away in the tropical heat of the north Amazon basin. British Guiana it had been then, Guyana now. I was a young officer in the Intelligence Corps, just out of the Royal Military Academy at Sandhurst, attached to the 1st Battalion, the Devon's and Dorset's, an infantry battalion sent to bolster the resident UK forces pending independence. The other infantry battalion, down in Georgetown, the capital, were the Buffs or, more correctly, the East Kent's.

We had been stuck 30 miles inland on the only major airfield in the country, an old staging post on the WW11 air routes to Africa, India and beyond, now a rather tired gateway from the new Guyana, to the world. It had a new name 'Timehri International', but that was about all that had changed.

The officers' mess at Atkinson Field, as it was then, had been inhabited by a cross section of people. Apart from the D&D's there were the usual assorted hangers-on: the teacher, a doctor, the resident Army Air Corps and Royal Air Force chopper boys and me - 'I Corps man', as I came to be known. The rest of the army called us 'the green slime', but here it was 'I Corps man'. Nobody seemed to know why and I didn't complain.

Of course, you can't keep nearly 300 men miles from the fun without trouble brewing. The powers that be, recognising this, allowed frequent visits down to Georgetown, the capital, at the mouth of the Demerera River 30 miles away. This invariably resulted in all hell breaking loose to the intense displeasure of the Buffs, whose comfy little sinecure GT had become, and who viewed the weekly invasion from the west much as the Romans viewed that of the Barbarians from the other direction. The conflicts were many and memorable. When not rearranging each other, the female population provided a gentle and far more satisfying distraction. Few amongst us had not succumbed.

So, here I am, with a lot of water under the bridge, now freelancing for Reuters, covering what passes for the latest exercise in democracy in these parts. In those days we had spent much of the time fixing up the elections so that Whitehall's chosen man, Forbes Burnham, got in. The old revolutionary Cheddi Jagen, whose efforts at civil disobedience, assisted by a hostile government in neighbouring Venezuela, and the reason we were there, did not.

Never let it be said that the British government couldn't play fun and games with elections if it wanted to. We collected ballot papers from non citizens, dead citizens, and quite a large number of the animal citizens, as I recall.

Still, all that's changed now. Cheddi's party has been re elected for the third time and things are as peacefully corrupt as they always are in these parts.

I'd come down to cover the latest elections about a week ago and, for nostalgia's sake, had stayed in the old Tower Hotel on Main Street, opposite the Booker store. For the same reason, I had taken to spending the evening at the Starlight Club on the coast road out of town, towards New Amsterdam. We had used it all those years ago and, like everything else here it seemed, very little had changed.

It was a pleasant place to waste away the time, until the summons home, looking out as it did over the South Atlantic rollers pounding what looked like white sandy beaches. Although, as I had found out to my cost one raucous night, those 'sandy beaches' were, in fact, pure Amazonion mud under a crust of salt. I'd sunk up to my hips in it, much to the delight of my dusky companion. Ardour-wise it proved to be something of a damp and smelly night.

It was on the second night there whilst enjoying the Demerara rum and coke (the coke still costs twice as much as the rum) that he came into the bar.

I put him in his fifties, tall and fit-looking, with those clear blue eyes that noticed everything. He didn't say much, just ordered the obligatory rum and coke and moved to a corner facing the door. By the second night we had got to the nodding 'Evening' stage. Each time he had stayed until about 2200, as though waiting.

I suppose the nosiness of the 'hack' eventually got the better of me because I finally picked up the drink and walked over. 'Mind if I join you?'

'Sure, take a seat.' An accent, hard to place. Transatlantic? Maybe something else.

'What brings you to this backwater? My name's Bill Slater, by the way.'

'Jim Kennedy, Bill, pleased to meet you. Why, I live here. We've got a place over near Bartica, on the Essequibo river. It overlooks the town from the east bank of the Cuyuni River. They join up there, you know.'

We shook hands and settled back. Somehow the silence had none of the awkwardness so common on these occasions.

He was obviously preoccupied with something. 'Actually, I'm waiting for a couple of old buddies,' he said at last. 'Something of a reunion really. What about yourself?'

So with nothing better to do, I dumped the lot on him: the Army, my time in what was then British Guiana, and the years with the media. He didn't say much, knew a few of the places in the country that I mentioned, said he had done a bit of flying himself, later admitting to 20,000 hours or so all over the world. But in answer to the obvious one of 'What the hell are you doing here?' his reticence returned.

I got a call from London the next day with orders to return. However, the next flight out was not until Friday so I had one more night to kill and, what the hell, why change old habits? Once more I resumed my place at the bar of the Starlight Club. Bill came in as usual, but it was obvious something had changed.

'Hi,' he said, parking himself opposite. 'Looks like my two mates are going to make it at last, any time as a matter of fact.'

Some time later the doors opened and two men stood for a few seconds, their eyes adjusting to the light, or lack of it. Jim called and they moved towards us. A more contrasting pair you couldn't imagine. One thin, about 5'11, the other 5'7 and built like a truck. One I thought English with a trace of the soft lilt of Ireland in there somewhere, the other was obviously Australian, and suddenly Jim's accent became clearer.

We stood and Jim shook their hands, turning to introduce me. 'Bill, these are two old buddies of mine. Digger here was our last flight engineer and Shaun, the other, pilot.'

Digger, the shorter of the two, stuck out his hand, more of a paw really, and gave the ritual bone breaker. 'G'day, mate.'

The pilot, a more reserved nod. 'Pleased to meet you.'

However, upon mention of my media connection, a distinct chill descended and each gave Bill a sharp look of enquiry. The old antennae, which had been sensing something for the last couple of days, now positively hummed. What the hell was all this about? These guys were up to something, or certainly had been. They were all from the same mould and from the look of them appeared to have plenty of money, but what were they doing here?

'Bill, would you excuse us? Me and the boys have some business to discuss.'

'Sure. Maybe I can buy you all a drink later?'

'Yeah, thanks.'

With that they moved to the back of the bar where, apart from the odd laugh from the Digger, the conversation was muted.

At the time it's difficult to know why you do some things. I was so sure that there was a story here that back at the Tower Hotel later I called London and said I needed a couple of days to check something out. Jerry, the features editor, was none too pleased but had enough brains to let me go with it.

So curious had I become that I was early at the bar that night, having spent the day gently digging around Georgetown trying to get a lead on anything to do with these guys. I need not have bothered as it turned out, because they had beaten me to it and by the look of them, the old rum and coke had taken a pounding. Certainly the welcome was a little warmer than the previous night's effort.

Jim called me over. 'Bill, your ears been burning? We've been talking about you. Word is you have been asking a few questions.'

Christ! How did they find that out so quickly? Feeling like a child caught stealing, my embarrassment was obvious and wasn't helped by the laughter it caused.

'Don't worry, mate, this is a small place and, as you can see, we are connected. Still, what is it you want to know? I guess the old journo nose has been twitching, has it? Well, as it turns out, this could be your lucky day. How would you like a story?'

I couldn't believe my ears. It just doesn't go like this. 'Okay, what's the catch?'

'No catch, Bill, it's just that we have a story to tell and we reckon it's time for the telling.'

So it began.

CHAPTER ONE

Trans-Pacific Airlines
Secret Board Meeting. Sydney, Australia

'We have a problem.'

'You bloody bet we have a problem. This whole crazy idea is falling apart, Meldrum, and I want out. You said we could pick up $5,000,000 each. The way things are we will be lucky to escape the nick unless we do a Skase.'

Mr Skase had been one of a number of Australian high fliers who had walked with the cash when things had got a bit tough in the 80s.

'Belt up, the lot of you. You were all for it when we started, so there's no bloody use whinging about it now. Unless we stick together, we're lost, so shut up and listen.'

Meldrum could be pushy when required and the predictable blast from the senator had needed an early stamp on, if only to stop the rest of them panicking. Not that panic wasn't justified, given the situation they faced.

The director of operations raised his hand as arranged, a nod from Meldrum and he began. 'As I see it, we are up for $25,000,000 at this stage. The problem is a note for this amount is due in the company accounts in two months and we can't cover it. The Bangkok business has collapsed, the properties would be lucky to get five. Any of you got twenty to put in? No? I thought not.'

The whining and grovelling began again, most vocally from the politician, as usual.

'Be quiet,' snapped Meldrum, with more confidence than he felt. 'There has been another development. We have been approached by certain interested parties in Thailand who may be able to help.'

The clamouring for more information and first signs of relief were gratifying. How easy it was to manipulate these bastards. The next bit might not be so easy, of course.

'Certain Thai interests have let it be known that they are aware of our situation and are willing to deal.'

'Deal – deal, how?' from the senator.

'I'm not sure but I am going to Bangkok tonight to meet them and find out. As I see it, we have no choice, so I want a clear agreement from you all that I have a free hand in this. Consider the alternatives before you say anything.'

Slowly the heads nodded assent. Easy, he thought, but Thailand looked anything but.

Bangkok

City of corruption, sex, deviation, all the delights of the flesh! A place where just about anything is possible, no job too big or too small. Here, there was always the man or woman to fix your particular problem. All that was needed was the word. A whisper on the street and eventually a meeting with the problem solver!

Or so it had been back in the heady days of the Vietnam War. It was a wide open town in those days, with fortunes made and lost, almost as fast as lives, and with about as little fuss. For all that, the place hummed and the street crime levels were low. Too many capable people there then, too many, really, had 'seen the elephant' and knew how to handle themselves. No self respecting thug is going to try and mess with a wired up young GI on R & R from 9 months 'over there' against North Vietnam's finest, at least, not more than once. It happened, of course; the boys got pissed, fell over, got robbed and worse. What usually followed ensured that that particular bar changed hands pretty quickly and another unidentified body was found in one of the canals.

In those days you could fix anything: wife giving you trouble, politician in the way, guns, tanks even aircraft wanted. Down to the seamy stuff, little girls, little boys, head jobs, hard jobs, you name it, all you had to do was find the right man or woman.

Things had slowed up after the war, of course, but the fixers were still there and the places of rendezvous. The public image of the place had been cleaned up some, but to those who knew, it was business as usual - a little slower now but 'b.a.u.' just the same.

Lucy's Tiger Den, then on Surawong Road (like a lot of bars in Bangkok it moved about a bit) had become famous during the war as the place to find the man for the awkward job. It was the chosen bar of the hard men. Not surprising, really, as Tiger Rayling, ex-Vietnam veteran had woken up late one morning after a monumental poker game to find he was now the not-so-proud owner of a bar and a girl called Lucy. Having made the switch from trained assassin to entrepreneur, Tiger naturally felt more comfortable with those he knew. While he very soon found his limited number of friends disappearing into the abyss of the war there was a steady flow of like-minded travellers to keep the business profitable.

The bar itself was unique in Bangkok, in that here, the only girls allowed were Lucy and her daughter. Here, peace and quiet was the rule. Conversations were always discreet, the music low, and the booths in relative darkness. In all, an atmosphere of mutual respect that comes from knowing that the other guy has been there. You didn't have to like the man, but this was not the place to settle scores, old or new. The occasional drunken tourist staggering through the door soon realised that the sudden chill in the air was not entirely air conditioning and usually left; with a little encouragement at times, but left just the same.

Francis Meldrum sat quietly in the corner, feeling distinctly uncomfortable. The obviously high levels of testosterone evident in the other customers was bad enough, but the atmosphere was hostile anyway. Already he regretted leaving the choice of venue to the man he was to meet here.

He was, in all senses of the word, a weirdo: 5' 6" on a good day, his chromosomes had been a mess from the day of his birth, to the extent that his sexual preferences were bizarre to say the least. This had caused him considerable difficulty at the military academy to which his father had sent him, in a last-ditch attempt to get things straightened out, to no avail. An incident in the showers had brought his already lacklustre military career to an ignominious end, much to the relief of all who knew him, with the possible exception of his father.

Undaunted, the young Meldrum had embarked on a career in business. Already brought up in a strictly religious family, he then joined the local business associations and so, with his now well established 'other connections', he had every base covered and was virtually guaranteed a successful career.

From small trading companies to an equally small airline, he had progressed to insurance, banking and even a government consultancy, making useful contacts on the way. Today found him along with the rat pack of fellow travellers he had collected on his corporate journey, as the chief executive of Trans-Pacific Airlines. He had been called in by the incompetent son of the founder, now deceased, to sort out the mess the airline was in.

As was his way, he had ruthlessly purged the organisation of all who had any idea of how things should be done and who could have asked awkward questions about phase two. This involved ensuring that the fortunes of one F. Meldrum and friends were considerably increased while the exercise in 'reconstruction' took place. Naturally reserves, purchasing, servicing and morale hit the bottom very quickly, but the profits soared and the share price followed.

The shareholders asked no questions about some of the more peculiar practices, in spite of constant rumours that 'something may indeed be a bit smelly in the state of Denmark!' And smelly it was because, for once in his life, Francis was in trouble. He and his cronies had dipped deep into the company cash to fund a large scale resort development in Thailand, with a view to selling it back to the airline as a package holiday deal at considerable profit.

The crash of the so called 'Tiger' economies had found them hopelessly overexposed to the tune of about $25 million. As the meltdown developed, they had become increasingly desperate to the point that they had been willing to consider anything. As is the way in Thailand, desperate situations soon become known and the problem solvers appeared.

He stood as the Thai approached, dwarfed and intimidated by his bulk. His proffered hand was grasped by the man, who unsuccessfully attempted to suppress the revulsion felt at the piece of 'wet fish' he found himself holding.

He sat opposite. 'Your problem, Mr Meldrum, is not insoluble. In fact, if you and your colleagues have the nerve, it can be turned into something quite profitable.' He began. 'You own an airline, I believe?'

'Well, I don't exactly own it, but, yes, we do control it. Why?'

'We have the need to transport large quantities of material around the world from time to time and your assistance in this could be quite lucrative. Obviously, not the full amount you need, at least, not at first, but if you are agreeable we may be able to cover that for you on the understanding that we have a deal.'

'What sort of a deal?'

'I think we should be quite frank with each other, don't you?' The Thai was quite proud of his English and liked to use what he considered sophisticated expressions when he could, although frankness and sophistication were not going to be

5

very high on the agenda in his dealings with this man, he thought. 'Your situation, as we see it, is that having invested $25 million in property here, you now find it is now worth only $5 million. Furthermore, the $25 million was, shall we say, borrowed from the company accounts in a slightly flexible way.'

Francis' mouth was dry. He was, of course, aware that these people must be well informed, but to have their situation laid out like that was not pleasant.

The Thai moved slightly, placing himself in the shadows and leaving Meldrum feeling even more exposed. 'We are prepared to provide you with sufficient funds to retrieve the situation for you and your friends. Of course, we will expect certain considerations in return.'

Here it comes, thought Meldrum. 'What sort of considerations?'

'As the CEO of Trans-Pacific, can we assume you have the ability to arrange the passage of certain items with, shall we say, discretion?

Meldrum said nothing, nodding a brief affirmative.

'In return for our considerable investment in your survival, we would require the movement of particular cargoes of a more sensitive nature from time to time'.

Again, a non-committal nod from Meldrum, but curiosity is a powerful thing and he could not resist it. 'What sort of items?' as if he couldn't guess.

A blank stare from the Thai chilled him. 'It will not be necessary for you to be informed. All that is required of you is that the goods are delivered where and when we say. You do understand that minor inconveniences like customs will have to be avoided?'

A spluttering protest from Meldrum instantly reduced to a strangled croak as the Thai's massive hand closed around his neck.

'You should be aware, Mr Meldrum, that your options here are few; you either cooperate or face oblivion. Do you understand?' Going blue, Francis managed yet another nod. 'Naturally, we would cover ourselves in this, Mr Meldrum. No doubt you and your friends will gather some courage when you return home; it is the usual way of things, we find. With this in mind, I should inform you that each consignment will be made to you personally, so any interception or loss will, of course, be instantly traced back to you.'

As the horror of such an arrangement sunk in, the blood drained from Meldrum's face.

'I see I have impressed you,' murmured the Thai. 'Good, as long as we understand each other! We will now discuss the first shipment.'

Again Meldrum was about to protest, silenced as much by the Thai's raised eyebrow as the slight movement of the hand.

'You have a freighter coming through Bangkok in five days' time. We will require space on that aircraft; one pallet of, shall we say, furniture, for your personal use, of course.' The Thai could not resist a brief smile as the look of alarm spread over the face of his companion. He continued, 'The furniture will be loaded in London. The aircraft will arrive here and experience mechanical trouble. We will arrange this. During that time certain things will occur. You do not need the details. All that is required of you is to ensure the aircraft arrives here and the crew are got out of the way.'

Meldrum, now totally controlled by the Thai, could only whisper that the crew would be no problem as they changed here anyway, and that all that was required was a delay in the call of the new lot.

'Good.' The Thai smiled; no warmth here, more contempt. 'I will leave you now. You are no doubt familiar with this city's red light district in Patpong. Can I suggest the Boy Girl bar in Patpong 3? The little boys are delightful!'

Francis flushed with anger. 'How dare you suggest?'

'We don't suggest, Mr Meldrum, we know. We know all about you. The apartment on your Coast of Gold, the private deals at company expense.'

Francis' jaw dropped and for once he was stuck for words.

'Close that, Francis – in this town it's not a healthy habit!' He got up and left.

Francis took ten minutes to control himself and followed. Where was that bar?

Room 688, Dusit Thani Hotel, Rama 4, Bangkok.

The Thai entered the room and shook hands with the Korean, nodding briefly to the other man.

'So, we have him?' speaking in English, their only common language.

'Yes, he is ours for as long as we need him,' said the Thai. 'I have encouraged him to the bar and the cameras are ready, so we will have influence in two directions. I think we can safely say Mr Meldrum is our man. If the discovery of the drugs is not sufficient, the film will be.'

'This is good! Our friend here, nodding to the man in the shadow, is ready for the other shipment now. When do you expect the aircraft?'

The Thai thought. 'If we proceed as planned and advise the Australian customs official we have of the shipment in, say, 5 days' time. He will approach Meldrum with the news of his imminent arrest in one week. A few hours to sweat and we will then offer the next part of the deal for his perusal; only the rough outline, of course. I will then make his position clear on the next day, with the films of his activities tonight as a further incentive, if required. I shall leave on Thai Airways the day the shipment is due out of here, that is 5 days' time. That way I shall be in Sydney in good time for our meeting.'

The third man, Arab in appearance, moved forward and, in heavily accented English, said, 'We require the items by the end of the month. I trust you can deliver at the agreed fee? Mistakes will not be acceptable.'

The Thai glanced at the man, 'No, four weeks will be sufficient.'

The Arab left and the two Asians settled with a bottle of brandy.

'The ship will arrive in three weeks from North Korea. The equipment will be processed by your people and moved to Utaphao airport. You are sure that the wheels have been oiled? My government will not look well on mistakes and you are already aware of our Arab friend's misgivings.'

The Thai looked balefully at the Korean. These communists were a pain in the arse, he decided, but the years had been good and the money exceptional. It seemed that as long as the Americans and the West were made to look foolish, they were prepared to do anything. This latest deal is really only an extension of years of shipping anything from jeans and condoms to AK47s, aircraft and ammunition to whoever wanted them. All that was required was a mutual hatred of the USA and the West. This deal would, however, probably be the last, he decided. Something this big should set him up for the rest of his life.

The Korean, as though reading his mind, stared at him and for once the Thai felt control slipping. A chill passed over him.

'We will require you to position to Bahrain with the aircraft, you realise that?' he said.

The Thai was surprised. 'But my part in this is over once the aircraft leaves Thailand. Payment was agreed at that point.'

'Things have changed, my friend. For something this big, we require you to see it through to the end.' The tone left no doubt .

CHAPTER TWO

Lucky Plaza guest house, Patpong 1, Bangkok

The pilot lay on his bunk in the third rate hotel they used these days. Certainly slipped down the ladder some from the main line, he thought. The air conditioning, never at its best, had given up in the early hours. Now bathed in sweat, he watched the flies chase the mosquitoes around the forty watt bulb that provided the sole source of illumination. It had taken him months to get used to this stinking heat all those years ago; not much chance of it now, he thought. Just lie here and leak.

Typical of the new order to tell them the flight was delayed, only minutes before they had been due to leave for the airport. Something to do with a cargo door jamming. Looked as though it would be a night flight after all. Rolling sideways, he grabbed the phone. 'Digger, fancy a drink? Call Jimbo, will you? I'll meet you downstairs in 30. I'll just call the office and see if I can get a time on this business.'

Bobby's Arms had been to aircrew what Tiger's was to the mercenaries; a crossroads, a meeting place and information exchange. Now things had settled back down to the long-haul crews on the South East Asia, Antipodes, Europe and UK run. As bars go, it was even more discreet than Tiger's, stuck as it was at the back of a covered car park off Patpong 2. As a result, the technical crews were left largely to themselves, apart from a little colour occasionally provided by the girls from the cabins. Even they tended towards the 'experienced' end of the business, enduring with amused tolerance the high levels of 'pilot talk' that were inevitable.

The three of them sat together, talking to a British Airways crew, casting glances at the women. 'Not many of them these days, especially on freighters,' muttered Digger. 'Anyway, we are so old we wouldn't know what to do if we did catch one! You just remember you were supposed to chase them!'

One for the road, they agreed then they had better hit the sack.

They eventually got out to the airport the following afternoon and bussed down to the southern end where the freight terminal was. Nobody seemed to know much about the reason for the delay and certainly the aircraft technical log did not enlighten them.

'Better give it a good look over, Digger.' said Jim, who was the captain for this leg.

He and Shaun took it in turns. It wouldn't have suited some of the fragile egos they had known in their time, but these two had been together for years and with Digger, the flight engineer, they were all but inseparable.

The departure procedures completed, they were airborne in forty-five minutes and heading south, the sun setting as they reached the initial cruising level of 29,000 ft.

The old 747, a clapped-out 100 series, rumbled through the night air. Mach .84 was the usual cruise speed for this model but this old girl used so much gas that economy cruise was nearer .81 now. It was on its seventh owner, a leasing firm in New York, whose only interest was in it making money. In fact, the aircraft was currently leased to Trans-Pacific to build up capacity. A few years ago an old crate like this would not have been considered by TPA but things had changed with the new order. The corporate raider had arrived and things had started their downward slide to the point where even this old aircraft was put on the books.

Spawned in mid-Pacific, just south of the equator, from the unholy alliance of heat and water, initially she was nothing but a splash of white on the photograph. But as childhood gave way to adolescence, the speed and size attracted the eyes of the satellite and she was given a name.

'Sandy' was next on the list and, as the elements combined, she showed that she was going to rival Tracy of 1982 in size and the toll she was about to take from those in her path.

The slow drift westwards soon picked up to 15 knots. The wind around the eye was up to 70 knots and increasing by the hour. Already the warnings were going out, the low lying atolls in her path bracing themselves for the onslaught.

Sparing nothing in her path, the inter-island freighter from Suva to Tonga disappeared without even a Mayday. Tonga itself soon followed, smashed beyond recognition with massive loss of life. It was later estimated that the wind gusts were up to 120 knots when she hit.

Gigantic waves had roared in, ignoring the reef and striking the low-lying shore, then sweeping inland with the tragic remnants of her victims carried at the forefront, to be dumped miles away, a broken mass of destruction.

To the west the ordeal was to come. In Darwin anxious eyes were glued to the televisions as the frequency of the bulletins increased to every 30 minutes. Here, most could remember Tracy and the exodus of those who could leave had begun. Those that remained worked long into the night to try and ensure something of the city remained if, as seemed likely, Sandy paid a visit.

It was the continental high that saved them. The pressure had been rising slowly for a week. Sandy hit the coast north of Cooktown, swiping that little town with the bottom edge of a storm that now measured 200 miles across and whose influence was double that. However, the massive high pressure system was unimpressed and as the two met it was Sandy who gave way, forced northwards on a track across Thursday Island and out into the Gulf of Carpentaria. Casualties were few; the mission on Thursday ceased to exist, but all had already been evacuated. Only the prawn trawler *Hope* succumbed, lost without trace because her skipper had failed to get the radio repaired when last in Weipa. He realised too late that this was not just another blow.

Sandy, now well out in the Timor Sea and tracking westwards, paid Darwin no more than a cursory visit. With the wind to the south touching just 70 knots, it was only old Harry, the resident drunk at the bar of the Territorian Hotel, who succumbed when a loose sheet of roofing iron neatly removed his head as he staggered home. Most agreed he would not have felt a thing. He was the only casualty.

As the pressure started to rise the winds near the centre slackened to a modest 90kts. However, she had one more date with destiny before the oblivion of the Indian Ocean overtook her, a meeting that was to change the lives of more people than could be imagined.

Darwin

Down at the airfield, Fred Calder was duty radio operator for the North West sector, covering the airways from South East Asia to the coast. The usual traffic, Qantas 2, Qantas 6, British Airways 11 and Sing Air 321 all for Sydney. Garuda from Bali and Jakarta to Melbourne, Trans-Pacific and Thai Inter from Bangkok to Melbourne, plus a few specials like the old TPA freighter.

Probably Jim again, he thought. They went back a long way and usually passed a minute or two in idle chat in the early hours. Tonight might be different, though, for as near as Fred could figure, Jim and the boys were not well placed to avoid this one. Better let him know, I guess. Let's see, Selcall code is DLCA. The static of HF gave way.

'Trans-Pac, 617 answering Selcall.'

'617 Darwin, that you, Jim?'

'Hi, Fred, what can we do for you?'

'617 Darwin, are you aware of the cyclone? It passed north of us and I reckon you're set up for a bit of meaningful dialogue with it on your present track.'

'617, yeah, we were told, but thanks for the tip. It looks like we're stuck with it, though; we don't have enough fuel to go around.'

A few more brief words and they ended the contact.

Timor Sea 33,000 feet

An oil line on number 4 engine had been damaged a few weeks ago in Singapore. Again, under the old regime of TK, the respected resident engineer, it would have been changed but now there were no spares and TK had long gone. Nobody really gave a damn anyway. So the damaged part eventually started to weep and then the first drops of hot oil came through, flowing aft and vaporising off the combustion chamber.

'We're losing oil on number 4, Jim'.

'Okay, Dig, keep an eye on it.'

'Jesus H. Christ! Fire in number 4,' Digger yelled, accompanied by bells and lights – the full catastrophe.

In the right-hand seat Shaun looked aft and could see the flames reflecting off the wing.

'Sure is alight, Jim.'

'Okay, number 4 thrust lever closed. Start lever cut off. Fire switch pull. How is it now?'

'It's still burning!'

'Okay, fire the bottle.'

Shaun's hand, already holding the fire switch twisted it clockwise.

Out at No. 4 engine, retardant was sprayed into the accessory bay and the fire died out. Unfortunately, now starved of the life-giving oil, the bearings on the fan rapidly overheated and it seized. The sudden slide, from 3,200 rpm to zero, ripped the fan off the front of the engine, throwing it forward, then sideways into the number 3 engine and the bottom of the wing, slicing into the main fuel tanks at the same time. Then the whole thing began again.

This was now life-threatening. The three men fought to extinguish the second fire on the number three engine and control the now hopelessly asymmetric aircraft. Fuel was pouring from the wing, and even as the fire in what remained of number 3 engine was extinguished, the slow glide to the two-engine altitude began, while clean-up operations and frantic radio calls took place. Digger managed to get as much out of tanks 3 and 4 in the damaged wing as he could but the holes were large, the leak massive. Before long they were down to what was left in 1 and 2 tanks on the left wing.

'How's it look, Jim?'

'Well, reckon the best we can do is the new Curtin Air Force Base near Derby, Digger. Did you manage to let Perth or Darwin know, Shaun?'

'I'm not sure. I haven't had a reply.'

'Christ! Derby, do we know anything about it?'

'No, only that it is an unmanned air base. Should be long enough, though; the F18s and the Air Force 707s use it. Anyhow, we don't have a choice, so let's get to it.'

Fortunately there were no passengers to worry about. TPA, itself having spent years avoiding freight carriage, now used these leased aircraft and crews retired from the main line to tap what had always been a lucrative market. The move to freight had raised a few eyebrows on the line after years of rubbishing by successive managements, but now regular runs had been established. The business proved to be as lucrative as the pilots had always said it would be. Certainly this flight was full, more's the pity as it turned out, because the high zero fuel weight had meant a minimum fuel plan.

Now roughly under control, if hopelessly out of balance, the crippled aircraft settled at 15,000 ft, the best she'd do on two, turning further south to put Derby on the nose. No contact with Perth or Darwin had been possible, Cyclone Sandy and the damage had seen to that. The Jeppesen airport manual told them, pilot-activated lights, no fire service; in fact, no services at all. As expected, it was unmanned, the nearest town was at least an hour away, if the road was open.

'Well, better not screw up the landing then, fellas, looks like a lonely night when we get there!'

'Love the positive vibes, Jim,' muttered Digger.

Jim managed a rueful smile.

Fifty miles out, the thrust on 1 and 2 engines reduced to idle, rudder trim moved back to near zero and the descent began. At twenty miles, the lighting is activated, no instrument landing system, of course, not even approach lights, just the two thin lines of lights shimmering in the hot and humid night air. No other ground lights anywhere. Thank God that bloody cyclone was still a few hours away

'This is going to be tricky. We don't even know which way the wind is blowing. I'll put the brakes on max, Jim, we don't have reverse and the spoilers may be damaged on the starboard wing. I guess we could try them but the way things are going tonight, they could get stuck out and we've got enough on our plate, I reckon.'

'You can say that again, Shaun,' was all Jim said.

Seven miles now, the gear is lowered and they are committed; flaps are now at 10 degrees with two more sections to go, but only half the leading edge slats had come out on the starboard wing. 500 ft, 1.5 miles, flaps roll to 20. The visual slope is very hard to maintain as there is no reference other than the two lines of lights in the darkness. Finally the flaps roll to 25 and the aircraft arrives. Landing is not a word used on these occasions. With no reverse thrust, the speed brakes on top of the wings are deployed and appear okay; certainly there is no tendency for the right wing to lift. In fact, there is very little tendency for anything to lift. Even so, the runway is eaten up at an alarming rate and the brakes are applied by both pilots. The aircraft judders to a halt with the runway end just under the nose. Digger, glancing over the vast engineer's panel in anticipation of further trouble, muttered, 'I'll give you a 10 for that one, boss'

'What's that, Dig? Out of, or Richter scale?'

'Richter, boss, definitely Richter.'

CHAPTER THREE

TPA CEO's Office Meeting. Sydney

'What! Where is it, then?' The chief pilot, Nigel Mainwaring, blanched under the combined hostility of the CEO and his Operations Director. Known for his aggressive and bullying manner and complete inability to understand the first law of industrial relations, the chief pilot had risen to his present position by carefully avoiding anything to do with line flying for thirty five years. Picked as the man to kick the line pilots' butts, he had been the worst chief pilot in the long history of TPA. His present problem was very confusing, though. The aircraft was not theirs, it was leased, and the legitimate cargo was insured. The three crew members were amongst the biggest troublemakers under his command and would be no loss, and the embarrassing element of the cargo would have gone with them. So what was all the fuss?

'As far as we know, it's either in the Timor Sea or on the ground in the north west of West Australia. The last Perth heard was that two engines were out and they were going to try for Curtin.'

'Curtin, what the fuck is Curtin?' screamed the CEO. Jesus, this was not going well, Mainwaring thought.

'It's an unmanned Air Force base near Derby, no facilities or anything and the weather is so bad at the moment a search can't begin until daylight, if then. Frankly, Mr Meldrum, I would be surprised if they made it.'

Francis looked at his chief pilot. 'We will have to get up there. Now, do you understand? I want an aircraft ready in one hour and you be on it or you're out, clear?'

The chief pilot, visibly shaken by now, nodded, his productivity bonus looking more shaky by the minute.

'Get out.'

After his departure, Francis turned to the operations director as he spoke. 'This could finish us if they find that stuff.'

The operations director agreed. 'The customs will have our balls.'

'Fuck the customs, you idiot! The Thais are expecting the stuff today, think on that for a while. We must get up there before the rescue people.' Christ, I am going to finish those three bastards once and for all if I get out of this, he thought.

Rescue HQ, Perth, 0600 Local Time

It went off the air at 2300 local time. Last known position was 200 miles NW of Wyndham, just on the edge of the cyclone.

That's already causing trouble for us; she's moving at 25 mph south westwards and will have covered the tracks by now. Poor devils, hope they made it to land. Curtin's the nearest and we've alerted what there is at Derby but it's really only one man and a dog. Word is that the dog is the smart one.

'He says he'll leave as soon as possible; the man that is. However, the roads are already almost impassable. What about the choppers at Port Hedland?'

'Yeah, spoken to them again. It's the bloody weather. They are all on the wrong side of it. We've got a Hercules moving up that way, but it's not good, you should know that. Probably won't clear for a couple of days. We may be able to get in at first light; that's what we're aiming for.'

'We had a call from TPA, the CEO no less, very agitated. Wants to get there himself for some reason. I've tried to put him off. Must say it's a change to see the man is so concerned about his people. Surprising, really; everybody says he is a little prick to work for. Anyway that's the situation. I'm moving what we have north so that we can react as soon as the weather breaks.'

We've got about another 5 hours' fuel for the auxiliary power unit, Jim.'

Digger had managed to get it going and, as a result, they had light for a while. Unfortunately, the HF radio had failed. 'Bloody typical,' was the comment.

'I suppose we may as well have a look around outside.'

So leaving the flight deck, they descended to the main deck and then, via the hatch, through what is always known as Lower 41, even though it refers to the even older 707 and is really the main equipment compartment, or MEC. They released the ladder, just aft of the nose wheel. It slid to the ground. All were drawn to the starboard wing.

'Jesus! What a mess,' Digger said.

'It's a good job we've got our superannuation, mate. Francis, the fairy, would have us paying for this.'

The other two just looked. The rear half of number 4 engine was still there, minus the fan shroud and compared to 3 it looked quite tidy.

The fan from the front of number 4 had obviously hit 3 in the middle of the right-hand side and damn nearly knocked it off the wing. The little red movement marks were way out of line. They had been very lucky, they realised. Even now oil and residual fuel was pooling under the wing.

'I don't think this old girl will be going anywhere,' said Shaun, looking at the starboard fuselage peppered with holes.

'I can see why the HF's failed. The whole aerial's gone,' said Digger. 'Plus a big chunk of wing tip, too. Didn't you notice that, Jim?'

Jim said nothing but wondered how the hell they had made it at all. With so much damage it was a wonder she had not broken up.

'No, I suppose not, come to think of it,' continued Digger.

'Do you reckon Perth knows we are here, Shaun?'

'I doubt it. All I said was that we were going to try and make this place. I guess they will check here first, but it will take a while.'

'May as well have a look around the cargo then, eh?'

Jim recalled many years ago in Mozambique that an occasional peek at the freight could be interesting. In those days it had been tractor parts which bore an uncanny resemblance to military weapons and the like. A little look couldn't hurt.

Back on the main deck, they moved to the first of the cargo bins. As expected, computers, car parts and all the usual things modern society can't live without. Until they got to the front bin on the right-hand side.

Digger, who was poking around in there, suddenly yelled. 'Hey, guys, come and look at this!'

The others joined him. Where the container sat there was a twelve inch gap between it and the aircraft wall. Here there was a large gash in the hull where a piece of fan had hit the side, penetrating the freight bin and its contents.

No wonder I had a bit of a job with the pressurization, Digger thought.

'Certainly no super now, mate. Get a look at this.'

Running out of the container was a small trickle of white powder.

'What the hell is that? Let's take a look inside.'

Lifting the curtain revealed furniture filling the available space and labelled.

'What's that say, Digger?'

Digger, struggling with his glasses, read the label.

'F.R. Meldrum, staff cargo. Special handling required. This looks decidedly iffy, mate.'

Jim looked at Digger. 'You know what it looks like? How do we check it?'

'I wouldn't have a clue what the difference is between heroin, coke or talcum powder, would you?' Digger grunted.

'I think we can assume it ain't talc, boss.'

'Yes, I guess so. What the hell are we going to do now?'

Shaun, who had stood back looking at the shattered container, moved forward.

'You know what this means? We've got the little bastard, don't you see? I mean, it's consigned to him. He must be up to something.'

'Nah,' said Digger, 'he'll wriggle out of it somehow, you know him. I reckon we should pass the info on and let somebody really nail him.'

'Okay, how?'

'We are going to be up to our eyebrows in this. The little shit is just as likely to try and pin it on us, isn't he? Anyway, who can we tell out here?'

'Look, Jim, the stuff is heroin, I think. As far as I can tell, it's only the legs of those small pieces that have been filled. How about we take them out and burn them in the bush? That way there's no evidence for Francis to use against us and we can inform customs when they get here. Francis won't find out the stuff is missing until later and then we can watch the fun. What do you think?'

'Yes, but make sure we get it all.'

Shaun climbed back up to the cockpit and flicked on the landing lights. They had another four hours of fuel for the Auxiliary Power Unit. He then returned to plan the removal of the ten pieces of furniture they reckoned had been tampered with. Unfortunately, Sandy, who had been gently rocking the old aircraft, decided to add about 30 knots to the wind and threw in torrential rain for good measure. Any outside work had rapidly become impossible.

'Okay, so here's how I see it: we get the door open as soon as the weather eases. We remove all the suspect stuff and destroy it. We close up and just act dumb. Then when we get to Sydney we let the customs people take it from there,' Jim said.

Shaun and Digger nodded.

'I know someone in customs,' muttered Digger, 'used to be shacked up with my ex wife's sister. Can't say I like the bloke, but he'd be somewhere to start.'

Jim, looking at the torrential rain through the flight deck windows, turned. 'I reckon that's about it for now. We'll get some sleep. I'll take the first watch, you two hit the sack.'

It would have been 6 hours later. The night had been horrendous. Even the old 747 had moved in the winds and rain that lashed the airfield. But gradually, as dawn arrived, the wind started to ease and the rain reduced to a light drizzle.

As the light improved, Digger, whose watch it was, stood in the doorway at left 1, stunned by what he saw. Apart from the runway with the aircraft sitting at one end, the entire landscape resembled an inland sea. Uncertain at first, he leant forward in the doorway, then moved back, calling up the ladder that gave access to the flight deck. 'There's an aircraft up there, fellas!'

The three of them stood in the doorway at left one, looking and listening. The wind was down to about 30 knots now and it had moved around to the South West still full of moisture, even though the humidity was dropping. The airfield had become a lake with a deceptively thin ribbon of tarmac stretching like an arrow into the north west. The engine noise that had first attracted them had disappeared, bringing a brief feeling of disappointment, which passed as an aircraft slipped silently from the overcast settling on the runway end 2 miles away. They strained to see what it was, realising as it turned that the company Gulfstream was about to arrive.

'Christ, Jim, how the hell did they beat the rescue boys?'

'I guess the weather is clearing from the east and the rescue is coming from Port Hedland, Shaun.'

'Damn, there goes our little plan, boys; we are going to have to play this very carefully.'

Moving from the stairless doorway 15 feet above the ground, the three descended through the forward equipment bay hatch to the ground, standing by the nose wheel as the

Gulfstream, dwarfed by the mass of the crippled 747, pulled to a stop 50 feet away. They watched as the internal air stairs extended, curious to see who their rescuers were. Meldrum's appearance brought forth a collective intake of air and a groan.

'Fuckin' hell, what's that little shit doing here?' whispered Digger.

None were into the modern touchy-feely things like analysing body language, but from the way his little legs were going it was pretty clear that Mr Meldrum was a bit pissed off. However, what really caught their attention were the three who followed him, unknown to them, but large unpleasant-looking characters. The pilot, whoever he was, remained unseen in the Gulfstream's cockpit.

At last Meldrum arrived. 'What the hell happened here?'

The three looked at him with contempt.

Jim moved forward saying, 'Yeah, that's okay, Mr Meldrum, we are fine, thanks, and the aircraft is in one piece, more or less.'

The barely-disguised sarcasm was at first lost on the little man. 'What I want to know,' Meldrum continued, 'is the state of the aircraft. Can it fly?'

Jim turned his back and walked to the starboard side with Meldrum in his wake. 'No it can't,' he said.

Meldrum was, for once in his life, speechless as he took in the devastation that had been the wing. However, recovery was quick. 'What about the cargo? Have you checked it?'

It took all their will power to control the reaction to the question.

'No,' said Shaun, 'but there are some holes up there, as you can see, so I expect there may be some damage inside. I expect pallet 4 will be the one to check.'

Digger could barely contain himself as Meldrum's face paled

Meldrum turned, 'You three go to the Gulfsteam and wait there, I want to inspect this myself.

24

He moved to the ladder, calling the 'gorillas', as Digger had named them, directing one to go to the other aircraft with them, and the other two to assist with the search. Jim hesitated, offering to accompany them.

'No,' said Meldrum. 'You wait in the aircraft. The chief pilot is there. He will debrief you.'

Turning, he ordered two of the gorillas to lift him into the hatch.

As the three of them entered the Gulfsteam, the chief pilot emerged from the cockpit, hand extended and with the well known greasy smile. None responded.

'Figured it was you. What the hell is going on over there, Nigel?' said Jim.

Undaunted by the sub-zero reception, the chief pilot responded. 'Oh, we were all very worried, the CEO especially.'

'I bloody bet,' Digger muttered.

'No, we left Sydney as soon as I could get this organised on the off chance we could get in. Luckily, we have a global positioning system fitted to this aircraft so it's easy to get into these places.'

Yeah, thought Shaun, remembering last night's drama, you can put it in the rich boys' toys but not where it's needed.

'Anyway, tell me what happened. You don't mind if I tape, do you?'

Jim turned, 'Yes, we do, in fact. Knowing the way this outfit works, we will wait until we get out of here before we put anything down, okay? Oh, and you can forget the voice recorder; we've cleared that, too. What I will do is give you a brief summary.'

While Jim told the story Shaun looked out towards the 747. There was no sign of Meldrum or the three thugs. Pity they hadn't managed to get the dope destroyed; plan B would have to take care of it. That is, as soon as they had figured out what plan B was, of course.

An hour or so later, a quieter, more controlled and infinitely more dangerous CEO appeared in the doorway of the Gulfsteam. Clearly, a decision had been made.

'Did any of you go into the cargo area?' Jim moved forward, 'Well, of course, we did. I told you we had to get on to the main deck to get out. You can't do it any other way, can you?'

'So you are aware of the damage inside, then?'

'Only what you can see from the outside. Why, is there something we need to know?'

'Absolutely nothing,' Meldrum said, holding each in turn with a malevolent stare.

Shaun and Digger waited.

Clearly, Meldrum was unsure, but equally, a decision had been made. 'The chief pilot and I will stay here and decide what to do next. You three are to go over to the 747 with my men here and secure the aircraft. After all, we don't know how long it will be here, do we? Once that's done, we will get you out of here.'

The three heavies glanced at Meldrum, who gave a slight nod, indicating with his head that they should go.

Nigel started, 'Is this really…?'

Meldrum swung round and snarled. 'I'll deal with this. You get up there and get ready now.'

The crew realised something had changed and, with a growing feeling of apprehension, they left the little aircraft and followed the three men across the tarmac towards the 747.

It was just a whisper at first, then a definite sound. The pilots heard it, then Digger, who, in spite of, or perhaps because of, the years around aero engines, said, 'Allisons! It's a Herc or an Orion.'

In front of them the leader of the gorillas turned and snarled, 'Come on, you lot.'

The first words he had said and enough to show he was certainly not an accident investigator.

The noise increased, passed over and returned. At the far end of the runway, the aircraft appeared, a C-130 Hercules, the mist of humidity flowing back from the props to leave four trails in the air, which suddenly turned into a wall of white water as propeller pitch was reversed on touchdown.

Slowly, the Hercules eased off the runway. Meldrum's men were now totally confused. Clearly, this was not in the plan.

Meldrum appeared at the door and called them back; whatever had been planned was aborted, or at least on hold.

The Hercules, its rear door opening before it stopped, moved to a position about 100 metres from the 747. A figure in khaki jumped off the ramp and began to walk over; more men appeared behind him.

Ignoring Meldrum and the heavies, the soldier approached the three flight crew, 'You blokes okay?'

A brief nod.

'Well, sorry we have been so long. There's been a hell of a flap on; the rescue people have been unable to get anything here at all, everything north of Port Hedland has been flattened. Needless to say, they dropped you guys down the priority list pretty quickly, being a freighter and all. You know how it is. We are only here because we had an exercise out in the Tanami desert southwest of Darwin and some guy called Fred Calder in Darwin operations insisted we check this place out, seeing as how we were behind the cyclone. Reckon you owe him a beer. Sorry, my name's Pete Westerman, by the way. We're from Swanbourne lines in Perth.'

Shaun looked up, ' You SAS then?'

'Yep, that's us. Eh, you a pilgrim?'

'No, but I worked with your mates from Hereford a long time ago. They spoke very highly of you boys.'

'Entirely mutual,' the young major said.

Meldrum, who had moved towards them, stopped, visibly shaken, this clearly not in the plan.

The SAS man turned to him, 'You okay? Who are you, anyway? We were told these guys would be alone up here – if they had made it, that is.'

Meldrum coughed and spluttered.

Jim introduced him. 'This is our CEO,' he said, 'come up here all the way from Sydney to rescue us.' The major glanced sideways, picking up the slight inflection of an unknown dispute.

Pausing, he said, 'Well, it seems you guys have a choice. You can come down to Perth with my mob or go home with this guy, but I know the rescue people want to have a word.'

Jim stopped him, 'No, that's okay, Major, we will come to Perth with you.'

Meldrum, recovering, objected. 'I think, Captain, you should return to Sydney with us. After all, we have a more comfortable aircraft and we will be there about the same time, and I really do need you to debrief us.'

'No,' said Jim, 'we go to Perth, the company can tidy this up later.'

Meldrum, mouth open, was silenced momentarily. 'Just remember who you work for,' was all he could manage.

'Nice boss you have there,' said the SAS man, clearly aware of the vibes, but still unsure what it was all about.

As they walked off, the major turned, 'Oh, Meldrum, I'll leave a couple of my troopers here to look after things, if you like?'

Meldrum turned. 'That will not be necessary. My men can do that after we have finished the inspection of my property. You may go.'

'Well, fuck you, too,' muttered the major. 'Come on, fellas, I guess some food and a shower is long overdue. It's about 3 hours away, so let's get going.'

They entered the back of the C-130 and three headsets were thrown their way. They sat on the most uncomfortable seats ever made and plugged in. No conversation was really possible and after a cup of hot sweet tea they each dozed off surrounded, as they were, by a dozen of the most lethal humans on the planet.

Perth

Twelve hours later, clean and feeling a little better after a few more hours' sleep, they met in the hotel bar.

Shaun started it, 'You know what I think? I reckon the bastard was going to top us and destroy the aircraft.'

Jim looked up, 'That's the feeling I had, too. Nasty, as I couldn't see a way out of it at the time, either. Nothing we can prove, of course. The sooner we get on to your ex's sister's bloke, the better, Digger.'

They had been there about an hour, conversation slowing as the real fatigue hit home. Comfortable as airline crews tend to be in each other's company, these men could almost have a conversation without speaking these days.

Pete, the SAS man, stood unnoticed in the doorway watching them. Christ, they looked tired. Now the Civil Aviation Safety Authority people and the scumbag press were after them. Still he had got them a few hours' peace as nobody knew they were here yet.

He had been in the duty room when the signal had come through that the 747 at Curtin had been destroyed, some reference to an internal fire while the owner's men had been checking it over. Still, nobody hurt, just a pile of metal now and a big insurance claim, he supposed.

He moved forward and they looked up with a smile of recognition.

Jim waved at a chair. 'Take a seat, mate. I guess we owe you a beer.'

'Thanks,' he said. 'Actually, I've got some news for you.' Finishing the story, he looked up, none seemed in the least surprised. 'Look,' he said, 'it's probably none of my business, but am I missing something here?'

They looked at each other in silent agreement.

Jim turned, 'Okay, Pete, you're SAS, right?'

A brief nod.

'We know it's not your area, but we could use some help and advice here. There is an unpleasant side to this.'

'Tell me more.' Pete, intrigued, pulled up his chair.

CHAPTER FOUR

Sydney

Meldrum sat in the Thai's room in the Sheraton just across from his own headquarters. It was a modern hotel built on a small island of land between two major roads adjacent to the airport. As such, the views out over the parallel runways stretching into Botany Bay tended to favour the dedicated aeroplane watcher. The meeting, while not pleasant, was considerably less alarming than he had anticipated. The loss of the drugs seemed not to worry the Thai, who had reluctantly agreed that the subsequent destruction of the aeroplane had been necessary. Now he sat and stared, apparently deep in thought, as Meldrum waited.

'You realise,' he began, 'that we must now start again. Your problems remain unchanged from that which existed in Bangkok. You are still in our debt.'

Meldrum nodded a brief and reluctant affirmative.

'Furthermore, your personal position is somewhat weaker.' A packet was thrown on the table. 'As you will see.'

Meldrum leaned to pick it up, realising this was not something he wished to see at all. Opening the envelope, he saw a series of shots of his last night in Bangkok, damning proof of his paedophilia and enough to destroy him. His hand began to shake.

'Settle down, Meldrum!' began the Thai. 'Just look at it as an extra insurance on our part. Should you honour your agreement with us, these need never be seen again, apart from your personal copies, of course.'

'Now, to continue... You are selling one of your aircraft to a buyer in the Persian Gulf, I believe, an SP. Is that the correct term?'

The SP version of the Classic Boeing 747 had, in its day, been the racehorse of that manufacturer's fleet and was generally well liked by aircrew as a result.

Meldrum managed a rather shaky 'Yes.'

'We will require this to be staged through Thailand for some cargo we wish you to ship to the Gulf for us. We need this to be done in about three weeks, is that clear?'

Another nod was all that he could manage. The inside information these people had was intimidating and the pictures were enough to put him inside for years.

'The crew will not be aware of anything, of course. It may even be necessary to dispose of them eventually, which brings me to the next point. You gave no indication as to whether the three who landed in the desert knew of the cargo?'

'I don't believe that they did,' said Meldrum, but I was about to remove any chance of that when the bloody army arrived and I could do no more. However, I think they are ignorant.'

'Ah! I am afraid you are wrong there. They have spoken to customs and advised them of the drugs and made the connection with you. Of course, no evidence makes the case impossible to proceed with, but it is another unfortunate development for you.'

'How do you know this?'

The Thai smiled without warmth. 'We have our connections, Mr Meldrum. Unfortunately for them, the man to whom they spoke is on our payroll. He has advised them to keep it quiet as the lack of evidence makes a case impossible. He has told them you will placed under surveillance. Naturally, they will have to be dealt with eventually. Perhaps you have some ideas on this?'

Meldrum's mind rapidly realised the solution suggested. 'We could use them to deliver the aircraft and...'

'Exactly, the problem will take care of itself. Good, you are as cunning as they say, Meldrum. My congratulations. Now you must deal with your people. I will be here for a few days and you will be informed of any special requirements in due course. You will, no doubt, be interested in the financial inducements we are prepared to offer?' 30 minutes later, the Thai finished, leaving Meldrum with the ghost of a smile. 'You may go now.'

Meldrum rose.

The Thai stopped him. 'The pictures, Mr Meldrum, are yours.'

Meldrum grabbed eagerly at the packet and left, his hand shaking.

3 days later, boardroom, TPA, Sydney

They sat waiting for the CEO, aware only that there had been developments.

Meldrum entered, nodded, moving briskly to the table head. Calling them to order he began.

'Right, things have been moving along quite nicely for a change. That bloody business at Curtin was successfully contained by destroying the aircraft and we stand to get a nice little windfall from the insurance. There is one little problem there, which I shall come to.'

Having dealt with a number of mundane matters, the operations director who, as always, had been primed to ask the right questions, raised his hand. 'Have the crew got back and do they know anything?'

Meldrum turned: 'Yes, they have and they are the problem which will need to be resolved. However, what I have in mind will take care of them. As you are aware, we are disposing of the SP It will also bring us a significant bonus with the extra payment negotiated, outside the published price. Can't let the shareholders in on everything, can we? This aircraft, currently being converted to VIP interior, is due to be handed over in Bahrain in two weeks or so. Our Thai friend has indicated an interest in a one time charter to the Persian Gulf from

Thailand, at an extremely attractive rate. In fact, gentlemen, at a rate which will go some way to clearing our little problem and as the aircraft is going to be off our books by then, at no risk to us that I can see.'

Once again the operations director spoke. 'What's the cargo, or don't we need to know?'

The CEO smiled. 'I don't think that need concern us, do you? After all, the aircraft is not returning and, if I have my way, nor will the crew.'

The chief pilot, who until now had sat listening, turned. 'What exactly do you mean by that? Who's going to fly it?'

Meldrum could barely contain himself. 'Those three bastards did, as I suspected, check the cargo hold, and in the damaged container they found the stuff. Naturally, there was no evidence to back up their story, but it didn't stop them telling someone in customs. Unfortunately, that someone is on our Thai friend's payroll and he mentioned it to me, suggesting a little housekeeping was in order.'

The chief pilot paled. 'You mean to have them eliminated? Is that it? Why? They can't hurt us – they have no evidence. I want no part of this.'

There was a murmur of agreement from the table

Meldrum's eyes closed. 'I thought that might be a problem for you, Nigel. Okay, we will fix it some other way. For now I want you to arrange for those three to be briefed to take the aircraft to Bahrain via Utaphao in southern Thailand as soon as the modifications are completed. You can leave now.'

As the chief pilot and the rest of the board left, Meldrum waved the operations director to his seat, waiting. 'We are going to have to get rid of that man. He is weak, but the rest of them are listening to him and things could get difficult if he gathers support.'

The telephone in the penthouse suite of the airport Sheraton rang briefly.

Cabramatta, Sydney's inner west

Tran Van Sah had come into the country as a teenager in the late 70s with the wave of immigrants that the then Australian government had encouraged. Along with many countries in the so-called 'first world', this exercise in guilt-redemption was popular among the new breed of politically correct politicians with degrees in 'theatre studies'. As New Age university students it was about all they could manage, but they still saw themselves as the conscience of the world.

However, while Canada, for one, had been quite selective in the terms and conditions of its migrant policy, Australia, in a fit of misguided guilt or, as was suggested later, a cynical exercise in ensuring the then government's hold on power, had accepted just about anybody and, as a result, had ended up with a ready-made criminal class to add to the home grown variety.

Tran was now close to the top of this particularly unpleasant tree, running all the usual rackets: heroin, cocaine, protection and prostitution, along with a lucrative little sideline in disposals. The profits from these activities were all recycled through a legitimate funeral parlour and a pet food factory. The latter also provided a useful avenue for the disposal end of the business.

It amused him to reflect on the effect the consumption of pet food heavily contaminated with heroin would have on the dogs fed it by their doting owners. Most of the customers processed in this way were, of course, users who couldn't pay.

While it was through the heroin connection that he knew the Thai, this call concerned a disposal. He listened to the instructions, asking no questions. Even payment was not discussed. He simply replaced the receiver and waited for the fax picture of the 'client' to come through. Walking to the door, a stream of Vietnamese was directed at three of the group of young men who sat outside.

A detailed briefing session was followed by the issue of a weapon. Tran kept all the weapons under close control. These youngsters could not be relied on for too long, they would soon start using the guns on each other if he did not control them. As it was, the weapon he selected for this job was a sawn-off Browning A5 self-loading shotgun. He would have gone for something with more firepower usually, but he could not be sure where the hit would take place and the last thing he wanted was bystanders getting involved. Not that he gave damn about killing the white trash – he just didn't want the aggro that it would result in.

A lone rider slowly moved up to the house in Rose Bay, a select suburb on the south side of the harbour. It was a large, impressive residence. Obviously, this one had plenty of money, he thought, different from the usual garbage he was required to remove. He sat astride the motorbike under the trees on the opposite side of the road with the visor down, his mobile phone wired to an earpiece and microphone in the helmet. All he had to do was wait for the target to move and call the other two on their bike, then follow to guide them in for the hit. The information was that it was most likely that the man would make for the north shore so the other bike was placed on one of the slip roads to the Cahill expressway so that whether he used the tunnel or the bridge to cross the harbour they could intercept.

He watched as the car was reversed out of the double garage under the house. The driver glanced sideways as he passed, long enough to confirm the target. A quick call on the mobile to alert the hit team and he moved off to follow. It was not hard, the car moving at a modest pace to the freeway. As soon as he was sure he called again, telling the other biker that it was the bridge.

The hit team had sat astride their bike, visors up, quietly smoking on the roadside. Only when a police car passed had they shown any apprehension. Much later the young officer would only be able to say that the bike had been red and that the riders may have been Asian. As the dusk fell, they watched the car approach, their spotter accelerating and indicating as he passed. The target remained unaware. Fortunately for them, there is no toll on the bridge for northbound traffic, so the pair attracted no attention as they accelerated to follow the car. Now it was just a case of opportunity. It was not long in coming.

A Volvo driven by the usual north shore bimbo, more concerned with what her gene pool were up to in the back and her hair, than driving, looked up to find the windscreen full of the back end of the truck she had been following. She did what she always did and stamped on the brakes. The driver of the target car immediately behind braked as well, but not fast enough to avoid lightly touching the Volvo.

Watching from a position four cars back in the adjacent lane, the hit team seized the opportunity. The pillion rider quickly turned around, facing backwards. With a well-practised movement, he pulled the sawn-off Browning from his leathers. As the bike came alongside the now stationary car, the rider slowed, the gun held horizontal by his partner, aimed at the driver's side window.

The first shell was a single ball bearing designed to smash the window so that the next rounds of kangaroo shot, really only five smaller balls, could reduce the target to something resembling mincemeat. Three rounds was all that was required. The bloody mess that had been the chief pilot of Trans-Pacific Airlines slumped in the right-hand seat. The woman, for whom being hit in the back was something of a specialty, had leapt out of her car to abuse the driver, only to see the bike accelerating away. Then she noticed the horrendous sight in the front of the car behind her. The usual quite pointless screaming was not long in coming, although, true to form at the subsequent questioning by the police, her main concerns were the insurance claim and whether a further claim for trauma counselling for her and her brood was possible. She provided no useful information on the bike or its riders.

Neutral Bay, Sydney, 2000 hours

The three sat in Shaun's apartment overlooking the harbour. The message on the answerphone had been brief.

'Shaun, Nigel here. I must see you all, it's a matter of life and death. Meet me at your place at 1900.'

'Bloody odd!' said Digger. 'What's that creepy bastard want?'

Jim moved to the door as the bell sounded, to be confronted by a young policeman. 'Would you be a Captain Fitzgerald or Captain Kennedy, sir?'

'Yes, I'm Kennedy.'

'I'm afraid I've got some bad news for you. Your friend Mr Nigel Mainwaring has been murdered. We found this address in his car, so you were the first call.'

'What happened?'

'Well, sir, it appears that he was shot in his car by a couple of guys on a motorbike, at least that's what the bloke behind him said. They were on the harbour bridge. Caused one hell of a pile-up. Could you come with me to the station? We need some details and a positive ID.'

'Of course, but I doubt there is much I can tell you. Have you spoken to his family and Trans-Pacific Airlines?'

'Being done as we speak, sir,' said the young policeman.

Returning from the police station, they were none the wiser, apart from the fact that Mainwaring had apparently been stopped in traffic on the bridge when two men of Asian appearance on a motorbike had used a sawn-off shot-gun to kill him. It had not been a pretty sight . The late news carried a brief clip of the CEO of TAP eulogising on Nigel's worth, but no information on the killers.

'I've got a bad feeling about this, Jim.' Shaun turned to Digger. 'That mate of yours in customs is okay, isn't he?'

'Stuffed if I know, but as I said, I am not overkeen on him, but he is customs. Surely they are straight? Christ, what am I saying? I'll believe in Father Christmas if I go on like this.'

They talked long into the night. No matter how you looked at it, they reckoned there was little to commend the position they were in. Listening to the last words of the chief pilot again, it seemed obvious from the tone that whatever it was he had to tell them was likely to be a warning and that someone did not want them to know. If only Mainwaring had made it at least then they may have got an idea of what was known by Meldrum.

Finally agreeing that they were out of their depth, they turned to the only person who was likely to be able to help, 'What's the time in Perth, Jim?'

Jim, squinting at the clock, paused. 'About 2200, I think, Shaun. No daylight saving over there, as far as I know.'

'Okay, I reckon we call Pete.'

Shaun spent some time working his way through the telephone system until he finally got through to the switch at the SAS base.

'Swanbourne lines,' came the usual bionic voice so common on military exchanges.

'Can I speak to Major Peter Westerman, please? Tell him it's Captain Shaun Fitzgerald and that it's urgent.'

'I'm not sure we have anybody by that name here, sir,'

'Yes, you do. I was speaking to him 2 days ago, so be a good chap and don't piss me around. This is a serious matter. Shaun, anticipating the usual delay, waited for the inevitable dose of elevator music or the ravings of the local talkback radio programme that seemed to be the common device used to drive callers mad these days.

Eventually the operator came back on the line. Major Westerman had left instructions that if Captain Fitzgerald or one of his colleagues called he was to be informed immediately. This was being done and their number was being passed to him as they spoke. He would be calling back as soon as possible.

'Blimey,' said Digger, hearing this on the area phone, 'that sounds as though he is as anxious as we are about what the hell is going on here.'

They moved back to the balcony and waited.

CHAPTER FIVE

Boardroom, TPA

The operations director turned to Meldrum. 'I thought the TV performance last night was a masterpiece.'

Meldrum smiled, 'Yes, I think we have managed to solve a number of our problems. The removal of our reluctant friend has closed off one potential leak and there is no doubt that the manner of his departure will bring all the others into line, particularly that political creep we have with us. I think we are going to have to deal with him eventually as well.'

'I must say, the Thais are remarkably swift when it comes to the need for decisive action. It is a refreshing change to do business with decisive people'. As if we had a choice he thought to himself. 'Of course,' went on the operations director, 'we have to find a replacement. Can't have an airline without a chief pilot, can we? If the Civil Aviation Authority found out, they would be down on us like a ton of bricks and that is the last thing we need at the moment. Actually, I have someone in mind who I think would be ideal for the job.'

Meldrum raised his eyebrows. Now, I wonder what this is all about? he thought. Establishing a power base, perhaps. 'Who?' he said.

'Well, actually it's Nigel's deputy. He is utterly ruthless, hungry to the point of greed and desperate for the job. I think I can safely say he has none of Nigel's reservations and with the added bonus that he is loathed by the line pilots even more than Nigel was.'

'Sounds ideal. We should see him as soon as possible.'

'Well, I anticipated that and I took the liberty of having him wait outside. I hope you don't mind?'

Did you now? How very clever of you? Yes, I really will have to watch both of you, Meldrum thought.

The rest of the board were called in then and the matter of the new chief pilot was discussed briefly before Meldrum went onto the next item.

'Now, before we deal with that in detail, we have another problem. The senator here is, as you know, the chairman of a committee that is reviewing customs and excise procedures. I am sure you are all aware that this has been extremely useful to us in the past, something we are all very grateful for, Senator.'

Amid the rumbles of agreement, the object of this accolade glowed, for once receiving the respect he felt he deserved.

Meldrum smiled. How easy it is to manipulate these politicians.

'Another small problem has come to our attention from the Senator.'

Another nod of recognition and its reciprocating glow.

'It seems our tame customs officer has, how shall we say, been persuaded to change sides. It appears the men from Canberra have leant on him and he is now unreliable. What I intend is to make another call to our Thai friend. Can I assume we are all in agreement?'

The nodding heads confirmed it.

'Well, I think that will do for the day, gentlemen. Things are progressing nicely and once we have cleaned up these few loose ends I think we will have everything back to normal. The meeting is now closed.'

As the last of them left, Meldrum once again waved the operations director to a chair. 'I will just make the call and then we will discuss the matter of the new chief pilot. I must say I am going to enjoy telling that man that the screw-up is at his end for a change.'

The Thai had paid a considerable sum for these women. They were certainly not the run-of-the-mill hookers. Still, for what he wanted, he required imagination and that cost money.

They had just begun what promised to bring him to the very edge of sexual ecstasy, a position he expected them to maintain until he was ready, when the phone rang.

At first he tried to ignore it, but finally the incessant noise destroyed his concentration and, pushing the girl on her knees in front of him away, he picked up the receiver. The initial grunt was followed by a long period of silence from his end. 'I will take care of it.' was all he said.

The women knew the job was finished by the look of him, not that it bothered them. This John had paid a lot of money up front, but it was never going to be a pleasant experience, given what he had wanted them to do for him.

The older of the two stood. 'I suppose that's it then. We can't return the money, you know,' more belligerent than she felt. This one was dangerous and Tran had told her any mistakes and he would deal with them, too. Just the thought of that turned her pale.

'Get out' was all he said.

They needed no more than that. Grabbing their clothes, they left to dress in the lounge before making a rapid exit.

He sat there for some time, deep in thought, eventually making the call.

Tran, replacing the phone, was surprised. He had thought at first that the women had not satisfied. This was soon replaced by curiosity. Two in three days... maybe this business was coming unravelled. He would have to think about this when the latest customer had been dealt with. At least this one would provide some enjoyment; the requirement to extract information was always a welcome addition to the business.

As usual, nothing was said, and no fax was required this time as the 'customer' was known to him. The only extra requirement was that the man had to be collected as soon as possible. The pick up could be done that evening. The place of interrogation was ready as it always was, and he would take care of that himself.

The instruction to publicly display the results of his work posed a problem, but with a little thought he felt he could find somewhere that would suit. Clearly, the intention was to not only find out what the individual knew, but to then send a message to those for whom he worked.

TPA HQ

'Wheel him in, then.' The chief pilot designate was the complete opposite of his predecessor, short to the extent that even Meldrum could look him in the eye. He was clearly excited at his potential elevation.

Meldrum decided to establish the ground rules up front. 'Right, this job requires absolute loyalty, unquestioning obedience, and a flexible attitude to certain legal restraints. Should you be able to comply, the rewards will be considerable for the right man, and I am not talking salary here. There will, however, be times when you would be required to act in the company's interest, if you understand me. Failure to do so would not be in yours.'

The man looked up, speaking for the first time, in an effeminate falsetto. 'I think I can say that I am not bothered by these matters. Nigel was clearly not up to it. I am.' he said.

Even Meldrum was a little surprised. Arrogant little prick, he thought. Still, if he does the job… 'Right, to business. We are, as you know, selling one of our SPs to a Gulf state as a VIP transport and that it has been fitted out with a considerable amount of, shall we say, special equipment, something which has significantly added to the value of the sale, I might add.'

He neglected to mention that this equipment was on trial for a British defence contractor and that it was of a secret nature and, of course, not his to sell. 'We have a second contract involving the aircraft, transporting unspecified items from Korea, through Thailand, to the Gulf. This is a separate deal and the purchaser of the aircraft may not know about it.

The flight will leave in about two weeks, transit overnight at Utaphao, south of Bangkok, and then proceed to Dubai, where we will meet it. From there we move across to Bahrain. We, that is, you, the operations director and me, will then ensure the delivery of the cargo to a place to be advised, returning with a substantial reward for our efforts. It will then be returned to Bahrain for sale. Do you have any questions so far?'

The chief pilot designate looked up. 'Could you define substantial for me?'

Meldrum smiled. An interesting insight. 'Oh, I think six figures should interest you.'

'Yes, it does if it's US dollars,' another smile.

'Dollars, of course,' Meldrum said. 'Now, to continue. This operation has to be discreet. Clearly, the freight is, shall we say, sensitive and the delivery flight is a good cover. However, it is vital that no leak occurs.'

'I take it we do not know what it is?'

'No, you do not know, nor are you to enquire. It is not in your interests. Is that clear?'

'Perfectly,' he said.

Of course, I don't bloody well know either, he thought. That is why I am getting on the aircraft in Dubai. Denial is easier from a distance, Meldrum thought, and I will have a chance to check everything before delivery in Bahrain.

'To come to the business of who is to fly it. We have been having some difficulty with Fitzgerald and his two mates. That disaster in Western Australia cost us a lot of money.' Actually, it had cost them nothing, but it never hurt to lay it on when dealing with these aircrew people. 'Furthermore, our Thai friends were not best pleased at the loss of the cargo. This deal is, in part, the result of that mess. What is required is that you ensure those three operate the flight. We have other plans for them once the delivery is made. You can offer them a cash payment of say, $10,000 as an added inducement.'

'Yes, I can ensure that they do it and they will be no loss to me. Troublemakers all of them, relics from the past. I gather they will not be coming back?'

So direct, thought Meldrum. He doesn't seem in the least bothered by their potential demise. 'Probably not,' was all he said.

'Right,' said the new chief pilot. He had quickly assumed he had the job, 'I will arrange for these three to operate the aircraft to Utapao; night stop there and then on to Dubai. I suppose you would also want 3 tickets to Dubai, say, 2 days before?'

'Yes, that should be early enough, I think.'

'Well, if you will excuse me, I had better get on with this. However, before I do, would I be presumptuous if I gave you this?' a note was passed.

Meldrum glanced at it; a series of numbers. 'What is this?'

'My account at the Swisse Credit Bank. It's where I would like the, er, added inducements you referred to, deposited, if that's okay?'

Meldrum, surprised at the confidence, smiled. 'I think we can arrange that for you, can't we, Gerald?' looking at the operations director, who nodded, equally surprised at the speed with which his protégé had 'joined the team'.

As the new chief pilot left, Meldrum sat looking at the door. 'Good grief, Gerald, what a little shit. Almost as bad as us.' They both laughed. 'Of course, we are going to have to watch him, but for the moment he will suit our purposes admirably.'

Fivedock, an inner city suburb, Sydney, Australia

The customs officer sat alone in the small and sparsely furnished lounge. Nothing about the immediate future gave him any hope. Since the divorce he had rented this small flat, itself part of a line of old houses in Fivedock, an area of working class houses just west of the harbour bridge. Although the whole place was changing as the yuppies moved in, prices were rising and he realised that a move would have to be made soon. It was inevitable anyway now because they knew. Before he had been very careful not to draw attention to himself by spending beyond his official income, but they had found the hidden accounts and now he was working for the government again. It had been that or jail. The thought that his other employer may find out filled him with fear.

The apartment, 1400, next day

The telephone rang as they relaxed on the balcony at Shaun's place discussing their uncertain future and awaiting Westerman's call.

Shaun walked back out, having answered the call. 'That was that little prick Cyril Adamson. You'll never guess – bloody Meldrum has made him the new chief pilot. Perhaps old Nigel wasn't so bad after all!'

'Still, at least the sawn-off little devo has got somebody he can look in the eye at last; maybe that's why he got the job.' Digger muttered.

Jim smiled, 'Somehow I don't think so Dig. What did he want?'

'Well, it's interesting. Apparently the SP they are selling is about finished and it is to be positioned to the Persian Gulf. Bahrain, to be exact, but here's the curious bit: they want it staged through Utapao for an overnight, then a transit in Dubai for some reason. Picking something up was implied.'

'What's this got to do with us, mate?'

'Oh yeah,' Shaun continued, 'That's the other funny thing. They want us to fly it. Apparently, we are the only ones available and all is forgiven. At least, that's what he said. He said it was a contract job, cash on the nose. No sum mentioned, of course. I said we would come in tomorrow to talk to him if that's okay, can't hurt to talk, can it? Funny the way they picked us, though. I mean, we can hardly be flavour of the month with Meldrum, but Adamson said he asked for us specifically, even offering the cash bonus.'

Chief pilot's office

'Come in, sit down,' Adamson said. ' Now, as the new chief pilot, I want you to know that we want no cock-ups on this. You will be paid a large sum of money.'

'How large?' Digger interrupted.

'I'll come to that,' was the testy reply, never at his best with those he considered his inferiors, and these three were definitely that in his mind. They had not even bothered to wear uniform to see him and now the odious engineer had lit up a large cigar in his office, using the No Smoking sign to strike the match. Still, they won't be around much longer, so play it cool.

In the next hour or so, he explained what was required. The fee was $10,000, payable on completion. They sat and listened to Adamson.

Finally, Jim, who was the agreed spokesman, said, 'We want seventy-five per cent of that up front. What's the cargo, anyway?'

Adamson, trying desperately hard to control himself, said, 'I think we can probably manage that, but I can't see why you want it. As to the cargo, its just a shipment of machinery from Korea.' Even as he said it, Adamson could have choked, but the three got up and left without any further questions, apparently missing the gaffe.

They were to see the chief engineer who was preparing the aircraft for sale that afternoon, but as they walked across the car park Shaun said, 'What's all this about Koreans then, is that North or South?'

48

Jim growled, 'Jesus, this is starting to really stink. You guys remember Maria in Bangkok?'

They nodded. They both remembered the long and sulphurous time Jim had had with the strikingly beautiful and highly intelligent Maria Fernandez. She had captivated them all but only really had eyes for Jim.

'Well, I guess I never told you why that cooled.' Neither said a word and Jim continued 'Well, as you know, she worked for that Syrian bastard. What she didn't realise is that he had put her name on everything and that most of the business was in re consigning stuff that was made in North Korea so that it could be sold in the West, particularly the USA. Trouble is, it was all sorts of stuff. She knew about the jeans and the condoms, but when the CIA tapped her on the shoulder and mentioned the AK47s, the napalm, tanks and aircraft, all in her name, she had to get out quick, remember?' The three of them had managed to smuggle her aboard a freighter that was bound for London just ahead of the Thai police.

Entering the chief engineers office a little later, the man stood holding out his hand. 'Heard about the Curtin business? Sounds like you blokes did a good job bringing that old girl back to earth. Pity about what happened after; we could have used her for spares, if nothing else. Funny business all round, really, I still can't understand what happened. Still, I've been told from on high to butt out. Now, I think you will like your new toy, even though she's 20 years old I think you will be impressed.'

They moved into the hanger reserved for long-term jobs and stopped dead. The SP sat there, magnificent in black. In fact, it was all black with a satin sheen to it.

'Jesus,' said Digger, 'that's a bloody silly colour for a sheikh's shag-wagon isn't it?'

'Yeah, well, we tried to explain, but what the hell? They are paying for it, so I guess it's up to them. Anyway, the air conditioning will cope and it's not just paint. It's some special radar-absorbing compound, supposed to make the thing almost invisible from certain angles. Wait till you see the inside.'

Jim stopped. 'What are those things on the wing tips? Those fuselage antennae are new, aren't they?'

'Yes, they are modifications requested by the new owner. The cylinders are chaff dispensers and the extra antennae are part of the ECM stuff we have put into her. The electronic gear is that stuff we got from the UK company; they installed it as a trial. They have flown it around a bit but things have been quiet for a couple of weeks, something about modifications. I must say I am a bit surprised Meldrum has got their agreement to sell it on. What the hell an Arab would want all that stuff for, I can't say. Maybe he has WWIII in mind! Still, it's all paid for, so who cares? Come on up, I'll show you the inside stuff. I think you will be impressed.'

Three hours later they left, not only impressed, but a little confused as to the exact function of their new toy. The main deck was much as one expect of a VIP transport, but the upper deck area aft of the flight deck was a complete electronic counter measures control console and very impressive.

Returning to Shaun's apartment, they were met by the SAS major.

Pete Westerman had been waiting for their return. Apologising for the communication cock-up, he explained that he had been summoned to Canberra, to speak with the Australian Security Intelligence people to be exact. At the mention of the overseas branch of the intelligence service, the three gave him their undivided attention.

Apparently, they were aware that a new drug flow into the country from Thailand was beginning, and they wanted to monitor the flow and trace it back to the source. They had been unaware of the Curtin business, but it was not reckoned to be the main method of getting the stuff in. From Westerman's report, the amounts had been too small.

However, they had instructed the SAS major, now reluctantly attached to ASIO, The Australian Security Intelligence Organisation, to use the three of them to see if they would provide any more leads on the Thai /TPA connection.

He was, in fact, disobeying orders by telling them all this, but as he said, he was a soldier, not a spook, and he was not in the habit of shafting people he now considered friends.

As he finished, Jim glanced at the others, receiving a nod from each. 'I'm afraid things have moved on a bit since we spoke last and we are all getting a little edgy about what's going on.' He explained in detail the developments since the murder of the chief pilot, to the meeting with the new boy and the reference to Korea that Adamson had let slip.

'Korea, eh! North or South? I wonder if the spooks know about that? I'll bet they don't.'

'Our feeling was North,' Jim continued. 'We have some previous experience with something like this,' he went on to explain 'This could be something quite unpleasant: North Korea using a delivery flight to ship something up to the Gulf, destination unknown. A one-off, totally deniable operation on an aircraft which is not going to return. You can see why we are a little apprehensive, I guess.'

'Sure. Aircraft doesn't come back, crew don't come back, right?'

'You got it.'

'There is something else you should know,' Pete continued. 'That ex-brother-in-law of yours, Dig. You were right to be suspicious. His people put him under observation for a minor complaint and they found large amounts of unexplained cash. Anyway, they pulled him in and it was pointed out that a twenty-year stretch was likely. The creep apparently near crapped himself, so when it came to the deal he positively jumped at it.

'You guys were right, there is a strong Thai connection. The one they thinks is the boss man has been down here on a visit. It appears he may have had a meet with our old friend

Meldrum. The receptionist at the hotel is pretty sure she saw them together. Of course, they are all chuffed to bits with the thought that they have got someone on the inside; it's been passed up the line as a major coup.

'He also blew the whistle on another nasty piece of work operating out of Cabrammatta. This one is Vietnamese and apparently runs the stuff they bring in on to the streets. Word is that he also takes care of the housekeeping and disposals. Anyway, the Feds are on to it now.'

Westerman continued, 'Leave it with me. You say it's a few days before you go? I will get back to you after I have spoken to Canberra, see if they know anything specific about this, although I doubt it. I bet the mention of the Koreans will rattle their little cages. See if you can get a lead on the cargo. In the mean time I think we are going to have to arrange to be in Utaphao for the night stop. Is it possible to get some of us on the aircraft for the run-up to the Gulf?'

They looked at each other and Jim began. 'Yes, it might be. We could take you on as a couple of performance engineers out of Sydney.'

'What do you think, Shaun?'

'I guess the Digger here could use a little help; after all, it is a completely new ship. Right, leave it with us, but Adamson said two days, so be ready.'

Fivedock

They had watched him leave for the airport at the same time for two evenings now. The bike they used was the same that had been used for the job on the harbour bridge, a red 750 cc Kawasaki. The city was full of them; it, like the two young Vietnamese who sat on it, drew no attention. The passing population didn't give them a second glance.

He walked, as he always did, to the corner of the street where the bus stopped that would take him to the station. The train to the airport was due 5 minutes after the arrival of the bus. From there, 15 minutes would find him at the international terminal, starting a ten-hour shift checking bags and papers, the inevitable result of his current situation. Tonight would be different, though.

The taller of the two bike riders spoke quietly into the radio and the dark saloon that had been waiting in the side street rolled slowly into the road, on the same side, silently approaching the man from behind. A further transmission from the watcher confirmed that they were alone. The car accelerated quickly and stopped just in front of the walking man. Both doors on the near side opened and without a sound the walker was forced into the car.

Once in the car, the struggles started. The syringe was thrust roughly into the neck and the man quickly passed out.

Tran used the funeral parlour for these interrogations. It was well away from the populated areas and the mortuary was beneath ground level. The inevitable noise that resulted from some of the disposals caused no problems as a result.

He was looking forward to the evening's sport. There was a sensual delight in knowing that whatever you wanted to do to the victim, ultimately he would be destroyed; the only question was how long he chose to make it last.

They had brought the unconscious customs officer into the morgue, cutting the uniform off his body and dumping him on to the table used for embalming.

Tran often thought how appropriate it was. Fitted with the usual drains for the fluids and waste of the embalming process, it was tailor-made for the business of torture – at least the style of torture he was expert in.

The man gradually came out of the drug-induced sleep, realising before full consciousness returned that something was terribly wrong, becoming aware of the fact that his arms and legs were both restrained, the arms pulled tight above his head and the legs spread wide and similarly tied. The fact that he was naked took a little longer to sink in, but as it did the full horror of his situation was confirmed as Tran moved into his field of vision.

Barely controlling his bladder and bowels, he managed to croak the inevitable query.

Tran leaned forward, the garlic on his breath causing the man to turn away. 'You are here to tell us everything. You have changed sides once too often, my friend, and you will now pay. The price is to be your life, the time to collect it is a matter for us to decide. To start with, we will give you a little demonstration of what is to follow.' Nodding to the other man in the room, a large set of bolt cutters was handed to him. 'You see these? Well, we are going to start by removing small pieces of you, just so you know what your situation is. We are not interested in questions yet. That will come later.'

The two men moved behind his head. He felt the first of his fingers forced into the jaws. What followed brought him to the edge of unconsciousness. Each time the pain neared the level of blackout, a bucket of icy water was thrown over him, followed immediately by the removal of another finger. He could feel the urine and excrement leaving his body as he lay there. Both hands, or what was left of them, were now numb with pain.

Tran brought the ten digits into his field of vision, laughing as his colleague lined them up on the heaving belly.

The interrogation followed; the man told them everything.

It wasn't much and when Tran was satisfied, the tape was stopped. 'So, that is all you have to say, is it? Well, we believe you.' He smiled as a look of relief passed over the victim's face, pausing to reassure before continuing. 'Of course, it means that now we can really start to enjoy ourselves. We have always wondered just how much we can remove from a body before death comes. We will find out tonight, I think'. He laughed as the stinking body on the slab wreathed in terror.

It took them an hour to butcher the man. By the time it was done, all fingers and toes had been neatly removed and large areas of the skin on the abdomen had been stripped away. The screams this and more had caused led to a piece of wood being forced into the mouth until the final act.

This required positioning a mirror over the barely-conscious man, set so the victim could see his genitals. They paused so a degree of awareness returned, assisted by yet another bucket of icy water. As the eyes opened, the vision was a puzzle until Tran's hand, holding the cut-throat razor, appeared. Once again, the pointless struggling began as Tran began slowly cutting through the soft tissue, neatly removing everything. He moved up to the still-conscious man, forcing the bloody mass into the mouth before the inevitable screaming could begin.

Bored now, Tran muttered to his companion in Vietnamese, and the large needle which was used to sew up the bodies after an autopsy now roughly stitched the mouth around the organ that protruded grotesquely from it. At some stage, death came at last.

Tran had decided that Centennial Park should be the place of display. The mutilated body, together with all the removed pieces, was unceremoniously dumped into the old coffin used to collect the bodies of the more orthodox customers. It was then taken to the van. Tran instructed the men that the body was to be hung there as an example, as had been ordered by the Thai.

CHAPTER SIX

Jet base, Sydney

They spent most of the next two days going over the specialist equipment on the aircraft and slowly realised that this was really a military aircraft now and, if it all worked, all but invisible to radar.

As it was, Meldrum, the operations director and the new chief pilot all left the next day and the insertion of the 'specialists' was no problem.

The chief engineer was there to see them off but asked no questions, understanding that at times it was best not to know. The three of them had spoken long into the night after the SAS major had left, coming to terms with the fact that whatever happened in the next few days it was going to be the end of their time in Trans-Pacific, and probably the country. It would be impossible for them to return, nor did they really want to; the business had changed too much for them. None had any real ties any more and they were all long overdue for a move. However, some rather rapid planning had been required to ensure they came out of this okay. Each sensed that their $10,000 was not going to go far.

A detailed plan was made with a number of options built-in to take care of the variables that were expected, even to the extent of ensuring that Pete Westerman was looked after, as he was coming along as one of the specialists. If all went according to plan, they would all be considerably better off in a week. Better off or dead!

Jim had spent over an hour on the phone calling Miami . As soon as he was done, Shaun also made a call. Old favours, owed in some cases for many years, were being called in.

Nobody objected. Having set up the connections, they both raided the chart store, pulling the Jeppesen's for the Arabian Sea, North Africa and the Central Atlantic.

Digger had spent most of his time going over the new systems on the aircraft. After familiarising himself with the new avionics, he dropped down into Lower 41, checking the hatch that enabled the forward hold to be reached in flight. It was a feature that was not well known and it could prove very useful in the next few days. Just to make sure, he spent some time attaching layers of padding to the inside surface, such that anybody in the hold would be unaware of its existence.

The following day, a message was received from Meldrum in Dubai.

'What the hell is he doing there, Shaun? I thought we were going to Bahrain after Utaphao. Why do we have to stop in Dubai?'

'That's right, Dig. Anyway, the deal's on; we are to proceed to Thailand tomorrow, so we had better let Pete know.'

They boarded the aircraft the next day. It had been parked in a quiet corner by the chief engineer, sensing the need. Only he and the tug crew were there.

He moved towards them. 'Good luck boys. Its been fun.'

Jim put out his hand. 'Thanks for looking after us all these years. I guess you know we probably won't be coming back.'

'Yup, figured that. Wish I was coming with you, in a way, wherever it is, but, you know... the wife, kids an' all. Anyway, you take care now. It looks as though you've got some insurance,' he said, nodding to the stairs, where the 'performance engineers' were in the process of boarding, carrying a long box. 'Not that I've seen anything, of course.'

'Yeah, probably best you know nothing.'

'Anything I can do, you know where to call.'

The other two shook his hand, then moved to the stairs and entered the aircraft. They didn't look back.

'Ground, Trans-Pac 101, taxi' Shaun, again in the right-hand seat, called the tower.

No start clearance had been required, as where they were parked was airline land.

'Trans-Pac 101, ground, you are clear to taxi for 16. Right via golf, and the bravo loop, are you ready to copy the clearance?'

As Jim waved to the ground crew, the chief engineer, standing by the tractor that had pushed the aircraft out, gave one final wave.

Shaun wrote the airway's clearance on to his pad, checking that it was as expected and what they had set up. 'Ground, Trans-Pac 101; be advised the aircraft is not in company colours. Er, it's black.'

As they moved clear of the hangers into full view of the other traffic there was a fair bit of ribald comment as to what they should do with it, racial insensitivity being a frequent feature, eventually the tower controller who was clearly having trouble keeping it professional, called a halt.

Within a few minutes, they had started the take off roll and, as light as she was, they were soon at the 6,000 ft required before the right-hand turn to the west could be made for the last time. Each looked out to the north at the city, alone with their thoughts, aware that it would be a long time, if ever, before they would see the place again.

Settled in the cruise at 35,000 ft, the initial level was again higher than usual as the SP was a high performer anyway and at these weights they would eventually climb up to the service ceiling of 45,000 ft. For now, flight level 350 put them well over the rest of the northwest-bound traffic.

As things settled in the cruise, Digger mentioned that the two 'performance engineers' should be briefed on the below main deck area, but before he could move, Pete said he needed to talk to them about another development.

'There have been some rather alarming developments, fellas,' he began. 'You recall I spoke to you a couple of days ago about your reluctant relative, Dig?'

Digger nodded.

'Well, I'm sorry to have to tell you he has been topped. It seems the opposition got wind of the fact that he had changed sides, and they decided to make an example of him. This happened last night as near as can be figured. They found him hanging in Centennial Park. The thing is, they had worked him over with what looks like a large knife before he died. Feeling is, he would have told them everything he knew, while he could talk, that is. They did the usual thing and stuffed his tackle in his mouth at the end. He was found in the early hours by some hooker on the beat. Scared the bejesus out of her. They have her in custody for now, so the newspapers haven't got hold of it yet. They are going to sit on her until they see what this is all about. Told me to keep it under my hat, but I reckon we are all in this together. Anyway, sorry, Dig.'

'That's okay, mate, I never did like the guy. Still, I wouldn't have wished that on him. How did they get on to the fact that he had changed sides so quick?'

Not for the first time, Pete reflected that there wasn't much these old guys missed. 'Interesting question, and one that has got quite a few people worried. It appears there may be a high-level leak somewhere. The information that we had turned him was only known to me, my boss and the top level of the department, which is about four people, I think. Oh, and Senator Jeffries, the minister. Thing is, there is a suggestion that Jeffries may have some dealings with Meldrum and that's making everyone uncomfortable.'

Jim, sitting sideways in the seat listening, looked up. 'Doesn't exactly make our position too good either, does it? I think we will have to be even more careful about what gets passed back to Canberra, don't you, Pete?'

'Yes, I think we must make sure nothing gets back that can be used against us. Fortunately, I can use Perth without going through Canberra. I guess you three have a little contingency plan of your own, eh?'

'We do have a little emergency scheme but we had intended to deal with it later, if that's okay?'

Digger again mentioned the need to show the hold and the ECM gear to Pete Westerman and his mate, the SAS sergeant at the Curtin rescue who had been introduced as Longstop, with the added advice of not to ask why. So, leaving the cockpit, they descended from the upper deck, using the spiral staircase to the forward cabin.

On the left side of the floor, the carpet was pulled back, revealing the hatch to the lower electronics bay. The two SAS men followed Digger down the ladder to the right-hand rear bulkhead. Pulling hard on the recently installed curtain, he opened the hatch inwards-revealing yet another curtain on the forward hold side, which had disguised the hatch's existence for them.

'Now we can enter the forward hold any time we like, as long as there are no large containers used. Somehow, I don't think that will be the case. We should be able to inspect the freight at our leisure on the run-up to the Gulf. Jim reckons about 6 hours, but he could spin it out to 7. Should give us enough time to figure out what's going on, eh?'

Westerman grunted, slipping through the hatch into the hold. 'Weird sensation, this,' he said.

'Yeah, empty aircraft in the air are a bit different,' Digger said.

As the aircraft approached Darwin, Shaun called up the Centre, advising the ground of their position. The instruction in reply was to Change to discreet bravo.'

This was the first result of one of the many calls made in the last few days. Shaun dialled in the new agreed frequency. It had been necessary to arrange it this way as any mention of an odd frequency change was, as matter of course, dialled up by every aircraft in the area, aircrew being generally bored out of their skulls and very inquisitive.

Shaun's call was answered by their friend, Fred Calder, on duty at the primary radar in Darwin as arranged. A series of switching exercises took place to ascertain just how effective the new equipment on the aircraft was. By the time they had finished, it was clear that with the normal transponder radar system switched off, the aircraft was all but invisible from the side and rear, even to the powerful ground-based radar in Darwin, and the return from the nose was much weaker than usual. Furthermore, this return appeared displaced on the radar screen in Darwin, in that whilst the aircraft was established on the 150 radial at 70 on the distance measuring equipment, its return on the Darwin radar was moved 10 miles to the east when Digger turned on one of the boxes down the back. None of them could explain this and it caused considerable interest on the ground.

The three of them agreed that a false image might come in useful in the next few days. A little more experimentation showed them that they could move this false return around to a distance of 100 miles from the actual aircraft position.

They left Darwin behind, after a few words of thanks from Jim to his old buddy in the radar room for the Curtin rescue and a few other things from earlier years. The SP slipped through the night, across the troubled island of Timor, joining airway bravo 583 then golf 463 to fly up the west coast of Borneo and out into the Gulf of Siam.

About 150 miles south of the coast of Thailand, Shaun requested a decent clearance from Bangkok control. With all the special equipment switched off, they had been on radar for the last 30 minutes.

The lights from the fishing boats glowed like jewels on the darkened surface of the sea as the aircraft dropped through 5,000 ft, well into the descent. They contacted the tower at

Utaphao for an approach clearance. Slipping into the last half of the published VHF Omni-Range procedure, they lined up with the Instrument-Landing System on runway 18, miraculously actually on for a change.

Jim called for increasing amounts of flap and then the landing gear as the aircraft slowed for the touchdown, watched in silence by the two SAS men seated behind.

Taking the taxiway to the old B52 parking area on the west side of the airfield, they could see in the lights that their arrival was expected. A group of decidedly military-looking vehicles were parked waiting. Jim eased the aircraft to a halt over the refuelling hydrants used by the USAF to fuel the B52s so long ago.

The marshal out front indicated that the wheel chocks were in and they shut the engines down. A set of steps was pushed up to left one door and the SAS men went down to open it.

Some rather unpleasant-looking locals entered the aircraft. The leader grunted words to the effect that a minibus would take them up to Sattahip, the local town and naval base. They should expect a call some time tomorrow evening. He did not seem to realise that there were two extra men in the crew, just thrusting a wad of Baht into Shaun's hand and waving them towards the transport.

As they left the aircraft, they became aware of a large group of men in the gloom. All appeared to be armed. They drifted towards the combi van which was to take them up to a hotel for the night. As the vehicle, which had been parked some distance away, moved up, other trucks had parked close to the forward hold.

'That's good, Jim, it looks as though it's all going into the forward hold. It would have been a bit awkward if they had used the back one, as we have no access.'

'Yeah, Dig, I was going to tell them they would have to use the forward hold for centre of gravity reasons, but it's much better this way. Trying to explain centre of gravity to one of this lot would have been interesting, I think.'

The guards, now totally engrossed in watching the loading, did not notice the two SAS men slip away into the night having first got the name of the hotel.

It had been agreed with the crew that, if possible, the two SAS men would remain at the airport to get as much information as possible about the Thai part of this business, and try and get an early indication as to what the cargo was. To this end, as the three flight crew boarded the combi, they had moved across the darkened tarmac to the perimeter fence and, finding a gap, eventually positioned themselves about 200 yards from the main gate. Here the intention was to hijack one of the two empty trucks to discuss with the driver, in robust terms if necessary, the late contents of his vehicle.

As they waited, they looked back at the aircraft, now surrounded by a group of heavily armed men. A number of large boxes were lifted into the hold.

'You know, Longstop, all this security would be reassuring if I wasn't bloody sure this deal wasn't as bent as its possible to be. As it is, we had better make damn sure they don't find us.'

Longstop, a man of few words, managed a grunt, which somehow more than expressed his agreement.

It was an hour later that the first truck approached the gate and the two SAS men moved forward to a position that would enable them to get into the back of the vehicle without being seen from the gate.

The truck approached the gate where a couple of unpleasant looking characters were on guard. The driver was ordered out and, as he climbed down from the cab with his back to the men, one leaned forward, dropping a thin wire over his head and in a cross-handed motion pulled the driver back onto his knee. The driver's hands tried pointlessly to pull at the wire, already sawing through his throat. No sound came at all, only a powerful fountain of blood as the main artery was severed. The killer managed to avoid this, demonstrating that this was far from being the first time.

The two SAS men had watched in horror, 'Fuck me,' was all Longstop could manage.

'I guess that puts paid to our idea of a hijack, boss, these bastards mean to close off all the loose ends.'

'Certainly looks that way, but we had better hang around for the second truck. You never know, he might be on the inside of this.'

'Certainly hope so, for all our sakes'.

The second truck had come along about half an hour later, only to have its driver eliminated in the same manner. The trucks were then turned and driven back on to the base, the bodies having been thrown into the back of the first one. The two SAS men remained in the ditch for a further 30 minutes, before moving back on to the airfield. With little more to do than watch the last of the loading, and hope for an opportunity to grab one of the loaders, which at this stage did not seem likely, they settled down to wait and watch.

Canberra, Australian Security Intelligence Organisation

The ASIO director sat looking at the others in the room. There were four of them; his own chief of operations, his American equivalent from across the road, the resident spook from the British embassy and the head of Customs and Excise.

This last was on his feet, completing a briefing of the situation as far as it was known. 'So, that's about it, gentlemen. We have established a link with Thailand regarding the drug flow. The murder of our informant was an initial setback, but it led us to the source of a considerably more damaging leak. As a result of that we are about to bring charges for complicity against the minister, with the usual escape option if he jumps ship.'

The director stood. 'Thank you for the briefing. Would you excuse us now? We have other matters to discuss. However, could I ask you to hold off on the Senator for a while? Picking him up right away would probably cause us some difficulty at this point in time.

The customs and excise man nodded, 'You'll let us know, then?'

'Yes. In the meantime, we will arrange to have him watched.'

As the door closed, the American and the Englishman looked at the director. Both were puzzled as to why they had been called to witness what seemed purely a local affair. In fact, given the embarrassment of political corruption, they were surprised to be here at all.

Sensing this, the director started, 'I imagine you are wondering why we asked you here.'

A slight nod from each in confirmation.

'Well, we have the beginnings of a problem, which, if instinct serves me right, is about to go way beyond our resources in terms of manpower and geography.'

He continued to brief them on the situation. He finished at the point that an aircraft was now in Thailand, being loaded with an unknown cargo which appeared to have begun its journey in North Korea and was destined, as far as they knew at the moment, for somewhere in the Gulf. At the mention of North Korea and the Gulf, both had sat up.

At least he had their attention, the director thought.

Inevitably, the American was first to speak. 'So, you have no idea what the cargo is, and the two SAS guys haven't checked in yet?'

'That's correct.'

'What about the three flight crew, what do they know?'

'As far as we can tell, very little. The SAS commander is under orders to mushroom them, but they do know about the initial drug shipment. After all, it was them that tipped us off. They would be bloody stupid not to have some idea that this is something bigger than that. It doesn't take a genius to figure out that if the business was drugs, nobody would go to all this trouble when you could just stick it on a boat in Karachi. No, I think we can be pretty sure these guys have a fair idea that this something else entirely.'

'And if this goes hot?' the American continued. 'They are part of this? Or are they, shall we say, expendable?'

'Well, we have had a look at that and, apart from an ex-wife or two, none of them seem to have anyone who would cause us difficulties if they disappeared. In fact, given the drug business, it would be quite easy to explain their disappearance, even if someone did ask and, as I said, that's not likely.'

'Of the three, two are ours. Kennedy and Digby were in Vietnam together, both decorated, according to the records. We are looking into that aspect now.'

'They were there in the Royal Australian Air Force and when they finished it seems they teamed up and went back with the then boss of Trans-Pacific. They flew on trooping contracts, Rest and Recreation, that type of thing. It's where TPA began. Apparently, the old man was quite something and these two were in at the beginning, good friends of his by all accounts. Of course, after his death, the son took over and proceeded to wreck it. Eventually, Meldrum and his gang moved in and, from the sound of it, completed the job.'

'The third one, Fitzgerald, is one of yours,' he nodded at the Englishman, 'or at least, partly so. As far as we have been able to ascertain, he has Australian, British and Irish nationality. He's certainly got all three passports. We haven't quite figured out how they got together but my guess would be Nam. Again there is some suggestion that your man was military of some sort.'

The Englishman, on who had said nothing so far, made a note to check him out. He coughed briefly and said, 'So, as I see it, we have to ascertain what the cargo is and, if possible, its destination, before we decide what to do about it.'

The director nodded and the man from MI6 went on, 'You say this aircraft is planned to go to Bahrain for sale, but you clearly have doubts about this being its final, or at least only, destination?'

Again a nod sufficed.

The American interrupted, 'Assuming this is something none of us is going to like, one way of dealing with that comes immediately to mind is to have them eliminated over the sea on the way up there. No evidence, no trace, and we have a aircraft carrier in the area.'

Not for the first time, the director thought how quick the Americans were to sacrifice the people at the front, particularly when they were not their own. 'I would remind you that flight crew aside, we have two of our special forces people on board.'

'Yeah, well, eggs and omelettes, director, you now how it is,' the American said

'Can I suggest that before we start disposing of everybody, we consider our options. I know I would very much like to know not only what this cargo is, but where it is going to end up. I think we should give serious consideration to arranging to get a look at whatever it is before it gets to Bahrain or wherever.'

Thank God for the Brits, the director thought. At least this bloke wasn't off on to WWIII like our other cousin. 'Any ideas?' he said.

'Well,' the Englishman continued, 'what makes it difficult is not having any idea what it is, and that has got to be a priority, but whatever it is, I'm sure we would all like to know were its going to end up and to do that we have got to get access to the aircraft to add a little something to the cargo. Now heading, as they are, for the Gulf, the place that comes to mind is Muscat in Oman.

'As you know, we maintain a sizeable presence there and we could arrange to have the aircraft inspected if a reason for a diversion can be found. I will have to enquire as to whether the required bugs and some specialist personnel are there, but if I get on to it right away, we should have time. I would think it would have to be some on-board technical problem that is the reason for the diversion. Anything else will arouse suspicion. In the meantime, director, I think that you would be well advised to sweat that senator of yours. He seems to be the only one who may know something.'

'Say,' continued the CIA man, 'who is the guy buying this aeroplane anyway?'

The director glanced down at the file in front of him. 'From what we have been able to find out from sources in the company, it is being sold to a company called Gulf Arab Imports. A Sheikh Anwar Sulliman is the name we have.'

The American paled, 'Oh, shit,' was all he could manage.

The Englishman spoke, 'This has just got very serious indeed. Do you know who Sulliman is? No, clearly not. Well, it is thought that he is a cousin of Osama Bin Laden. Need I say any more?'

The telephone rang and the director snatched at it. 'I thought I told you I was not to be disturbed,' he snarled, then stopped and listened intently for what seemed an age. Replacing the receiver, he faced the two of them. 'I am afraid it seems they, whoever they are, have beaten us to it again. Senator Jeffries has just been found in a hotel room in Kings Cross in Sydney. His throat was cut and his body mutilated. From what my people could see, unlike the customs informer, there appears to have been no preliminary torture, so they are assuming that whoever did it was not interested in making him talk – and from that you can deduce they already knew everything he did. The opinion is that it was done as an example. The manner of mutilation I leave to your imagination, but I can say talking would not have been an option.

'Sod it! That shuts down our last lead. All we have left, then, are your two men and the flight crew. We really must get back to your people and see if they have found anything out about this cargo.'

'Yes,' said the director, 'We will turn up the heat a bit when they call in next, which should be in about six hours. Leave it with me. In the meantime, it would be helpful if you each briefed your people of the potential problem, and you,' to the MI6 man, 'call your people in Muscat, putting them on some form of alert.'

'Okay, but I will need to know what the cargo is as soon as possible. Might pay to run a check on this Fitzgerald character as well. I don't think the flight crew people are going to be a problem, but it won't hurt to check.'

'Yes, and we will dig around some more with our two.'

The three men got up and left, leaving the director sitting there. Something was bothering him, something from the past.

It was the Vietnam thing that had got him thinking. Picking up the phone, he left instructions for his head of operations to return. If nothing else, he would clean up his own back yard in anticipation of the howls of outrage from the politicians at the violent demise of one of their own. He was only too aware of how insecure they all were, and if they thought that a senator could be eliminated in this manner, their immediate reaction was inevitably who's next? It would not matter that he was a corrupt bastard and that he got what he deserved. What was important was that their fragile little egos were restored

CHAPTER SEVEN

Utaphao, the Airfield

They had waited for about half an hour and then decided that it was pointless to stay. Moving back towards the hangars to the west of the runways, they came across the two trucks that had been used to bring the cargo in. So with nothing better to do, they entered each in turn. The first got no more than a cursory look, being quite empty, but the second still had the bodies of the drivers in the back. It was as they were searching through the clothing of the second one that the rear curtain was pulled back to reveal a young Thai male.

The boy's jaw dropped at the sight of the carnage and he turned to run. Fortunately, Longstop was quicker, grabbing him as he slipped off the ladder he had used, pulling him into the back and silencing him with a blow to the back of the head.

'Christ, that was a bit of luck,' Pete said. 'Hope you haven't put him out for too long'

'Nope, he will be back up any minute, you watch.'

With that the young Thai groaned and opened his eyes and, as memory returned, the fear showed, changing to horror as the two bodies were seen. As his eyes focused, his attention was entirely on the nearest one and he began to sob, holding his head and rocking back and forth. 'Pichai Pichai,' was all he said, the tears flowing down his face.

Pete glanced at Longstop, 'Thai's one of yours, isn't it? What's he saying?'

'Bloody hell, I think it's his older brother.'

'Poor little bastard. Still, we had better make it quite clear it wasn't us, so get to it, mate.'

Longstop sat beside the boy and talked slowly and softly at first, then with some force. The boy gradually relaxed a little as he realised that he was in no danger.

'We must get out now. Bring the kid, Longstop. We can talk some more when we are away from here.'

They hauled the boy to his feet and as he looked again at the body of his brother, the weeping began again. Longstop put his arms around the child and eased him out of the truck.

On reaching the ground, they moved as quickly as they could to the perimeter fence, none too soon, for the new truck drivers returned just as they passed the corner of the hangar.

'Okay, here's how I see it: we get this young fella away with us and then see if he can shed any light on the cargo. Best bet would be to get to the hotel in Sattahip, that way we are all together then, and the communication gear is there, so we can get anything he has off ASAP.'

A grunt was all that was needed from the sergeant to confirm.

As they moved away from the airfield, Longstop spent the time gently questioning the boy. Doing it on the move ensured that the child answered spontaneously, it was an old trick.

To get to the town they had moved as quickly as possible to the main Bangkok coast road. There they had hitched a lift in a truck, posing as a pair of aging backpackers, the young Thai as their local mate. He was still in shock and said nothing. Fortunately Longstop's Thai was improving with use and the driver was not much interested anyway.

By the time they reached the hotel the crew were using, the two soldiers had been awake for 30-odd hours and were feeling the effects. Fortunately, the young Thai had settled down and sat quietly, aware only that the two were not going to do him any harm.

Jim opened the door at the first knock, surprised at the third body, but saying nothing as he moved aside to let them in, grabbing the phone to call the other two as an update was obviously due. The SAS men slumped wearily on the sofa, pointing the young boy to the corner furthest from the door, where he sat wide-eyed, saying nothing as Shaun and Digger entered the room.

Pouring two large Scotches, the crew listened to the events of the night. Only the murder of the two drivers caused any reaction.

'I've got to get all this on tape and down to Perth now. With any luck, they will have some news from that end. Either way we need to know what is happening and the kid's info is going to light some fires down there, I think.' Pete began to fix up the small tape machine that Jim had carried in for him, and with which he would send the pulse message to Perth.

Longstop sat beside the young Thai. In faltering phrases, the boy repeated what he knew and then lapsed into silence, only to burst out that he thought the boxes had Chinese or Japanese writing on them and were something to do with guiding a rocket. He had used the Thai word for firework but as Longstop said, it was highly likely the poor little bugger had never seen a proper missile. Longstop suggested Korean but got only a shrug in response.

As the Major completed the tape, adding this last piece of information, he turned on his mobile and dialled the number. As soon as the line opened, the high speed tape sent its message and in the mundane exchange of pleasantries, it was just about undetectable. While the innocent conversation continued, the tape began running again as a message was received. Clearly, there had been developments at the other end.

Running the tape back and pressing 'play' bought the voice of the SAS man's commanding officer into the room. Canberra had fully briefed him and he passed on the state of play, including the fact that the high-level leak suspected had been eliminated by the other side. He ended with the requirement that until they knew exactly what the cargo was, it was impossible to plan a response, so they were to arrange a diversion to Muscat where a team of experts was being assembled. The manner and reason for the diversion was left to them, but as they would be obliged to inform Meldrum, the cause was to be such that suspicion was not raised.

Shaun and the others discussed this and Digger's plan proved the simplest and most plausible. What he suggested was that they tell Meldrum that a double flame out had occurred and that contaminated fuel at Utaphao was suspected. The delay in Muscat would probably be about 12 hours, long enough to give the people there time, but not enough to give Meldrum the excuse to fly over from Dubai. They would emphasise that the Utaphao stop was his idea anyway, so he was responsible for the problem. Reliable fuel supplies should have been arranged.

Having decided this, they began discussing the demise of the senator. Clearly things had really started to get rough at that end, too. Although it seemed as though the rats were fighting among themselves, it was clear that these people were to be taken very seriously. As if that had ever been in doubt!

The SAS men were just dropping off when the mobile began its call. 'Christ, that was quick. I bet it was the bit about the missiles that got the bastards going,' Pete said.

Sure enough, the message stressed in no uncertain terms the need to confirm this and find out the country of origin, concluding with the advice that US and British agencies were now involved and that they were to cooperate with both.

With little more to do until the planned call time in eight hours or so, the two soldiers settled down to grab some sleep. The Thai boy remained absolutely still in the corner of the room.

The call came at 1800, with the advice that they would be picked up in an hour. Shaun shook the SAS major's shoulder. He slowly opened his eyes, groaning.

'I thought you buggers were supposed to light up immediately.' Shaun joked.

'Oh, sod off,' Pete muttered with a smile.

They discussed what to do with the boy and settled for a wad of Baht and promise of pain and suffering if he mentioned even seeing them. The memory of his brother's death at the hands of his ex-bosses was thought to be enough to keep him quiet. Even so, they waited until the transport had arrived before they slipped him out of the back door.

Fortunately, it was a different driver so the extra two bodies drew no comment. The truck drove them to the base of the control tower, where they could file their flight plan. As it stood, the instructions were to proceed direct to Dubai with the eventual destination of Bahrain. Shaun, in the left-hand seat for this leg, told the driver to take the Digger and the other 'engineers' out to the aircraft to do the preflight and check all was okay while he and Jim went inside.

At the counter, where in years gone by countless young American pilots would have stood, they began the business of checking the plan that had been sent up from operations in Sydney. The weather in the Gulf was good at this time of year and a glance at Muscat revealed that it to would be no problem.

As they were completing the formalities, the door opened and an evil-looking local with an M16 slung over his shoulder walked in. He was followed by a large fat man whose appearance was straight out of an old Hollywood gangster movie. Even the smile and out-thrust hand did nothing to reduce the image that this was a thoroughly unpleasant character.

Shaun ignored the hand and said nothing.

The smile disappeared as quickly as it had come and, in almost perfect English, he announced his intention to fly with them to Dubai with three of his men, pulling a signal of authority from his pocket, written by Meldrum in Dubai, as he spoke. In fact, the signal said these people were to be treated as VIPs and extended every consideration.

Shaun handed the paper to Jim, who eventually said, 'Well, we have no cabin crew and unless you have arranged your own food, none of that to spare either. Oh, and you can forget about the cannons as well, we are not going to have any weapons on the aircraft, right.

The Thai turned to his gun toting bodyguard and, in burst of rapid Thai, gave him the good news. It was not well received.

The question of food had apparently been anticipated, so with the matter of the guns apparently resolved, they could think of no further excuse to refuse carriage and they reluctantly agreed. The Thai moved off to talk with the three men, who were obviously the ones who were going to accompany him.

Shaun turned to Jim and said, 'Okay, mate, I'll fix this lot up. How about going out to the aircraft and telling Pete we will have guests? He will probably want to set things up for them.'

Jim nodded and left the planning office to walk across the tarmac to the aircraft.

The Thai and his man waited, watching Shaun complete the business of filling the flight plan, gathering and reading the weather and latest notices that may be applicable. He was spinning the time out to give the four on the aircraft time to make the expected arrangements.

Jim called Pete and Longstop over.

Digger was well into his external inspection. 'Pete, we have a potential problem, a Thai guy, obviously one of the bosses around here, and, in fact, he sounds a bit like the bloke you described in Sydney. Anyway, he has turned up with a letter from Meldrum, authorising passage for him and three heavies to Bahrain with us. We figured you might want to rearrange a few things.'

Pete nodded to Longstop who opened the hatch in the floor in what had been the first-class cabin, to access the MEC compartment where their box of goodies had been stowed.

'What do you reckon, boss, the Brownings or the Sigs?'

Pete, standing at the top of the hatch, opted for the Sigs with silencers. Nothing too powerful wanted inside a pressure hull, he figured.

Now, tooled up and feeling more comfortable for it, they continued to the upper deck to commence setting up the ECM gear while awaiting their guests.

Pete was talking quietly to Longstop. 'This could be the break we have been looking for. If this Thai guy is as connected as Jim thinks, apart from inspecting the stuff in the hold, we have a source of info that could give us a lead on origin and destination.'

Longstop nodded. 'Of course, we will have to neutralise his mates first, soon after we get out of here, I reckon. That way he will have the maximum talking time.'

Shaun arrived with the Thai and his three bodyguards. The weapons, at least the obvious ones, had been removed. Neither of the SAS men were under any illusions about what they had hidden. In fact, as they moved into the light at the aircraft door, one of the locals appeared distinctly familiar.

Neither the Thai nor his men seemed surprised at the two extra men, assuming that five was a normal crew. Longstop showed them to seats aft of the door and showed them how to strap in, whilst checking out, what he could for any weapons.

'Boss, that guy at the back... ring any bells with you?'

Pete thought, yeah, he's familiar, but where from? 'Last night at the truck stop; he is the one who fancies himself with the wire, I reckon,'

'Yeah, you're right. Well, I guess that means he is elected number one, eh!'

'Works for me.'

Gradually the pre-start procedures were completed. Eventually, the front door was pulled closed and the stair towed away by the ground crew.

Shaun, in the left-hand seat, turned to Jim and Digger. 'Ready?'

A nod.

'Okay, start 4.'

The other engines quickly followed and as the last was stabilising at idle, the next checklist was completed. Jim keyed the VHF radio. 'Trans-Pac 101. Taxi.'

In broken English, with an appalling accent, the tower controller told them to taxi for runway 18. After yet another checklist Jim called 'ready' to the tower and received a clearance to depart. The instruction was to climb to FL150 or 15,000 ft and join the TANEK Standard Instrument Departure, reading this back and checking the navigation computers to confirm it was as they had expected.

Shaun lined up and called, 'Set thrust.'

The Digger leaned forward and set up the thrust levers as the old SP gathered speed and finally lifted off.

Light as she was, once again they out-climbed the evening's westbound traffic. Transferring to Bangkok, they were further cleared to climb, levelling off at FL350.

Pete came up and said 'We are just going to do a little housekeeping below. Best if you stay out of it for a bit.'

A nod from the Digger was the only reaction.

Pete and Longstop descended the spiral staircase, moving back into the cabin.

Pete, approaching the Thai said, 'Okay, would you like a drink or something?'

The Thais ordered a beer each and Pete moved into the galley to get them. Returning to the cabin, with Longstop standing behind him, he handed the three bodyguards a beer each, thereby ensuring that they all had one hand occupied; stepping back a couple of paces, he dropped the fourth can in the aisle. All three glanced down as he bent to retrieve it.

Longstop, with a clear field, put one round in each of their heads. The last of the men, whipping round as his two partners slumped forward, was hit just in front of the ear, causing the eye to be ejected from its socket. The low-velocity rounds, further slowed by the silencer, penetrated but did not exit. Nice and tidy, Longstop thought, no gooey mess over the new seat covers.

Sixth sense caused their leader to twist around, but Pete's half-clenched fist hit him below the nose, snapping his head back. Unconsciousness rapidly followed.

'Hope you haven't killed him, boss.' Longstop mumbled.

'Yeah, me too. I never was as good at that as you.'

The three bodies were left strapped in. Longstop checked them over, pulling a plastic bag over each head to keep any blood off the seat backs. Apart from the garrotte around the collar of the one known to them, he found a small pistol of Russian origin, plus a knife, with similar stuff on the other two. So much for no weapons!

The Thai slowly came to, the blood congealing under his nose and, as the reality of the new situation sank home, began protesting, then threatening and finally begging.

This is going to be easy, Pete realised. After a couple of hours, he reckoned he had most of it, the odd piece of reticence discouraged with the sight of one of his men's knives.

Throughout, Longstop had been in the hold, and together they had a fair idea of exactly what was going down. Both of them agreed that the cargo looked suspiciously like guidance systems. The Thai had indicated something similar; neither could be sure, of course, but given the relatively small size and the information so far it was not difficult to come to the conclusion that they were ultimately destined for Iraq, as he had said.

Longstop stayed with the Thai, staring balefully at him to the point where the man was feeling very uncomfortable. Pete, having made a detailed tape of their findings, moved to the upper deck to begin communication with Perth. The aircraft was by this time approaching Delhi and had about two hours before the diversion was to begin.

The information, when it arrived, caused consternation in Canberra. The director, once again, sat in his office. The time, 0400 local. Opposite him, the CIA man and the Briton from MI6 listened.

'Jesus Christ,' shouted the American, we can't let them get hold of that stuff. Are you sure they are going into Muscat, because we need to be quite clear that should they try and get through, we will have to whack them. The carrier *Nimitz* is somewhere south of the Seychelles and I am going to get them put on notice.'

'Well,' began the director, 'I have no reason to think that will be necessary. Let me reiterate: we land them in Muscat, MI6 and friends look over everything, placing a few special devices and we then trace the guidance systems to their destination, which will give us a lead on the main launch sites of the rockets. Surely that's better than shooting them down, isn't it? We also know, apparently, now that you have had the decency to tell me, that we have the problem of the aircraft. Don't forget that this is a two-ball game, and we don't really know whether the two things are related. Logic says yes, but with the Arabs one can never be sure.'

The Englishmen nodded. They had had a private chat before the American arrived and agreed that every effort must be made to follow both leads, in spite of the cousins' desire to blow everything up.

'We will remove this Thai for further interrogation in Muscat. We are going to have to make sure Meldrum and the rest of them in Dubai do not suspect anything. Some story about changing his mind at the last minute. It will take them a few hours at least to find out that he left Thailand with the aircraft, even if they think to ask the question. The suggestion could also be made that, as a result of the diversion, he had got off in Muscat and disappeared. Should satisfy that end for a while. Remember this guy Meldrum will not be aware that the Thai is not on-board until the aircraft gets to Dubai, and if things are handled properly there, he will not be able to make any enquiries until they arrive in Bahrain.'

The news that the cargo was probably destined for Iraq and that the boxes contained missile guidance systems had shaken the American. On returning to his embassy, he had immediately spoken to Langley, who in turn had quietly discussed it with Tel Aviv. It was here that the American urge to shoot the aircraft down was laid to rest, for a while. The Israelis were most interested in the British plan to follow the guidance systems to the missiles. A squadron of F15s was put on standby, as were three B707 tankers. However, unknown to the others, on the suggestion of the CIA man, orders had been issued for CVN 68, the aircraft carrier *Nimitz*, and her battle group to move towards the coast of Pakistan at maximum speed, just in case.

Crossing the Pakistan coast in the area east of Jiwani on the border between Pakistan and Iran, the SP on airway A791W was now at 41,000 ft and approaching the point of diversion.

Jim, speaking on VHF with Karachi radio, called up with just the right amount of anxiety. 'Karachi, Trans-Pac 101. We have a problem!' He went on to explain they had suffered a double engine failure. Fuel contamination was suspected, and they required an immediate clearance to descend and proceed direct to Muscat via airway R462, which conveniently left the one they were on at right angles and would take them straight to the large airport at Seeb, just west of the capital.

The Pakistan controller very quickly cleared them to approach Seeb, wishing them 'A safe landing, 'insh Allah' (God willing), although quite what God had to do with it was never very clear to any of them. Still it was a kind thought.

The New Zealand controller on contract at Seeb approach vectored them for the Instrument Landing System on runway 26, handing them over to the tower 20 miles out.

Jim, 121.7, the tower frequency, already dialled, up began. 'Seeb tower, Trans-Pac 101 maintaining 5,000. Request straight-in approach.'

The tower controller, having been advised that this flight was a bit special, cleared them to land. As they completed the landing roll, he told them to exit at the next left and cleared them to the ground on 118.6. Jim selected the new frequency on the radio and the ground controller directed them to park in the secure area in the military compound on the southern side of the field.

As they taxied clear, a 'follow me' truck appeared off to the left-hand side and Shaun turned to follow it as Jim and the Digger completed the last series of checklists. In the main cabin, the Thai had lapsed into stony silence, wishing more than anything that he had ignored the Korean's instruction to follow this through to the end.

The stairs were pushed up to the door and Pete swung it open. Subdued military uniforms were evident.

A British army captain stepped forward. 'Andrew Mckintosh,' he said, putting his hand forward.

Pete grasped it. 'G'day, Pete Westerman. You come for this joker?' indicating the Thai with his head.

Mckintosh nodded. 'Or at least they have.' indicating to the two heavy weights behind. 'Going to see if he knows anything more as soon as possible. I don't envy him. These Omani blokes are very good at encouraging talking. What we really need to see right away is what you have in the hold. What's the best way in? We noted that they have got it sealed up outside so we haven't touched it. Apparently, we can access it from the top side?'

Pete turned to the forward cabin and lifted the carpet, exposing the main electrical compartment or MEC hatch.

'Down there to the right and through the hatch. We left it open for you.'

Mackintosh stood staring down the hole, 'Good grief, I never knew this was here, did you?'

Pete smiled. 'There's quite a lot I didn't know about these things until this caper started.'

The Thai, now terrified, the wetness evident at the front of his once-immaculate trousers, was hustled away by the two Omanis.

The specialists, just arrived from London, descended through the hatch to begin a detailed inspection of the cargo. Another team arrived with stretchers and the bodies of the three Thai gunmen were loaded on and removed. It did not take long. Nobody said a word.

Each box contained a sophisticated guidance system clearly designed for attachment to a missile. Ironically, they appeared to have access to the global positioning satellite system the USA maintained, which was in general use by airlines as the primary means of navigation these days. Even after this initial inspection, the engineers were becoming very concerned at the apparent potential of the contents of the hold. The leader was soon on the secure line to London and Canberra with the preliminary findings.

CHAPTER EIGHT

CIA HQ, Langley, Virginia

Nothing the Thai had said to his British interrogators provided the listeners with any comfort. The information, or most of it, was routinely passed on. In Canberra, the CIA man again wanted to have the whole thing shut down. Fortunately, his director in Langley could see that whilst there was always a risk, the benefits of the British plan, to follow the devices to their final destinations and thereby locate the missiles, were worth it.

The thought of being able to stand up in the UN general assembly and show those Third World creeps that Iraq was the pariah the USA had always maintained would make it all worthwhile. If, as he suspected, a connection could be made from North Korea to China or Russia, so much the better.

Furthermore, with the Israelis on hand to do the dirty work and bring the thing to a satisfactory conclusion, the missile part of the business was well covered. All that remained was the loose end of the aircraft and the Osama Bin Laden connection – and he had an idea on just how it could be used to solve that particular problem to his advantage as well.

Picking up the phone, he pressed the button for the secure line to his counterpart in an office on the south bank of the river in London. 'Good afternoon, Sir Robert.' After the usual pleasantries, he began to discuss the idea he had for the second phase of the operation: the destruction of the aircraft, ideally with Bin Laden aboard, but in any event, under circumstances that would do the maximum damage to his organisation.

The MI6 man listened with interest. After all, it was his men who would have to place the necessary devices. Adding a few ideas of his own, the conversation finished. As he leaned back in his chair, Sir Robert had to admit the plan was beautiful in its simplicity, and there appeared to be no way HM government could be implicated, so while the Arab lobby may suspect, nothing could be proved. Anyway, most of the hypocritical bastards would be glad to see the end of Bin Laden. He was, after all, a potential threat to them all.

After the briefest of meetings with the people from the Arab desk who were running the Muscat operation, he issued instructions that it was now necessary to have a bug placed on the aircraft. This was in addition to the individual units in the cargo. This last device was to include a means of destroying the aircraft if required. The fallback position, as discussed with the CIA director, was that *Nimitz* would cover the Arabian Sea end and the RAF the routes out of Bahrain to the west. Nothing was set in concrete until further information on the plane's final destination and purpose was known.

The information from the Thai's interrogation that a large sum of bullion would be coming out on the same aircraft he would keep to himself for the moment. The question of sharing with the cousins could be discussed later, from a position of strength. Certainly, HMG would not sneeze at a $30 million windfall. The peerage was looking more hopeful by the day.

Seeb Airport, Muscat, Oman

As soon as the inspection team had come on board and been shown around, the three flight deck crew had moved into the rear cabin to rest. Once alone, they began to review their situation. It did not look promising. Clearly, as long as the feds wanted to trace the final destination, they were not at risk, at least from official sources. The problem, which was becoming very obvious, was that should those sources change their mind, the future would turn very nasty, very quickly.

'I wonder how much these people know about the special gear we have on board, Shaun?'

'Well, the technology must be known to them; most of it seems to come from Western sources, anyway. The real question is do they know we have it, and that it works? We know Fred in Darwin isn't going to say anything and the chief engineer in Sydney is very much our way, so I reckon that even if they know the old girl has some special stuff on board, they probably don't know how good it is. I think we had better have a word with Pete and make sure he keeps quiet. We had better make sure none of those boffins get up on the top deck, as well.'

Digger, ever practical, spoke. 'I guess we won't need any fuel here, will we?'

'You know,' Jim said, 'I reckon we fill her up.'

The other two looked puzzled.

'I have a feeling this is going to turn nasty soon and we may need to get out quick. The last thing we want to have to do is land for fuel. I reckon the chances of us getting airborne again if it's gone bad would be just about zero. What do you think?'

'The landing weight in Dubai, assuming we go there, is going to be over the limit, but not by much, seeing as how we are just about empty and all these Gulf strips are at least 13,000 ft long so it shouldn't be a problem.'

'Agreed. I reckon that's the go,' said Shaun.

A nod from Digger and he moved off to arrange the fuel.

Hyatt hotel, Dubai

The news of the diversion had reached Meldrum a few minutes before and, in spite of the assurances from his new chief pilot, waiting at the airport, that the reason was entirely plausible, he was highly suspicious. A call had been made to Muscat to the local agent, giving instructions that he was to get out to the airport directly to check on the situation. He now paced the marble floor of his suite waiting for a reply. He had also made a long call to Bahrain, where his local agent there was operating under the instructions of the Korean, who, in turn, was finalising the delivery of the cargo with the Iraqis.

The plan was for the aircraft to be chartered through Gulf Arab imports as a UN relief flight to Baghdad carrying medical supplies, which were to be loaded in Bahrain. The usual inspections on arrival in Baghdad were anticipated and an elaborate exercise in sleight of hand had been developed to keep the inspection team away from the forward hold.

Ramada Inn, Bahrain

The Korean stood as the Iraqis entered the room, shaking hands with the agent from Bangkok and nodding at the other two, one of whom was obviously the leader. 'So we move up the ladder a little, he thought. So far all negotiation had been with the man opposite him, but from now on he guessed the small overweight individual at the head of the table would be running the show.

The meeting began as the newcomer spoke. 'We will expect you to accompany the cargo on its final journey,' he said.

The Korean, who had anticipated this, gently shook his head. 'No, that will not be possible. My superiors have expressly forbidden it. However, your concerns have been anticipated and we have arranged for substitute, shall we say, 'hostages' to be provided.' No comment was made, so he continued. 'We feel that the aircraft itself represents a significant guarantee of good faith. However, recognising your leader's desire for human insurance, we will send the airline chief and his staff with the shipment. I am sure I don't need to remind you that it is not in any of our interests to cause problems with this. We will expect the aircraft to return here with the required bullion on-board. However, we have no objection to you keeping Meldrum and his people until you are completely satisfied with your purchase. It is our intention to eliminate the crew as soon as they have delivered it to its final destination, anyway. The aircraft, as you know, is required elsewhere for purposes that will meet with your approval when they are revealed, which leaves Meldrum, his staff and our Thai friend to be dealt with. We would, of course, prefer to retain the services of the Thai, as he has total control over Meldrum and it could be useful to all of us in the future.'

The Iraqi, who had listened without interruption, began, 'That will be satisfactory. However, should there be any problem, you should not expect to see these Western pigs again, you understand.'

'That would be regrettable, but I quite understand. There will be no problem, I assure you.'

The Iraqi continued, 'As to the bullion, this will be loaded on to the aircraft without the crew's knowledge. We will provide a suitable security presence up to the point of handover. We have considerable influence here; there will be no problems.'

The Korean stood as the Iraqis moved to leave. He had considered mentioning the question of the unplanned diversion which the local agent had advised him of, but had thought better of it. These people were paranoid enough without introducing further doubt.

As soon as they had left the Korean moved to the telephone, dialling the hotel in Dubai. Meldrum, who had been made aware, by the Thai, of the Korean interest in the business and that it was them who would be handling the arrangements in Bahrain, at least until his arrival, answered on the first ring.

After the usual pleasantries of introduction, the Korean asked, 'Have you news of the aircraft yet?'

'No, but I have our agent going to the field and I expect a call anytime. In fact, I thought you were him.'

'As soon as it arrives, you will join it and fly directly to here where there will be a 24 hour wait before the next phase, do you understand?'

'That will be no problem. Er, our Thai friend mentioned a sum of money at the point of completion. When can I expect that payment to be made? You are, no doubt, aware of our agreements?'

'We will discuss this when you and your staff are here.'

The telephone was abruptly put down, leaving Meldrum looking at his handpiece and feeling distinctly uncomfortable. I will be glad when this bloody business is over with, he thought, already having made up his mind to cut and run with as much of the cash as he could lay his hands on.

Military compound, Seeb Airport, Oman

The technical team had completed the very rapid inspection of the cargo and had found only the guidance systems. While this was disturbing enough, at least it made the business of bugging the stuff a little easier, as they could assume that wherever the boxes went there would be rockets and they were not likely to be in a populated area. As a result, collateral damage from any retaliatory action would not be a problem, something that could have been more difficult had they found any nuclear, biological or chemical agents, given Saddam's predilection for hiding this stuff among his people.

Each of the packing cases had been examined and the latest and least detectable locating device had been placed inside the case of each guidance system. Furthermore, anticipating the suspicion of the Iraqis, these particular bugs were not giving out a continuous signal, which would have made them vulnerable to a sweep. They were only going to be activated by satellite signal when it was thought that sufficient time had elapsed for them to have left the aircraft and be en route to their destinations.

One final device, the most powerful one, with an explosive charge attached, had been placed on the aircraft in the forward hold adjacent to the aircraft's centre wing tank. This, the last to be placed, was as the result of a direct instruction from London. Detonated it would destroy the aircraft completely, but in the meantime, once activated, it would enable Washington and London to follow the aircraft's movements.

At the last moment the leader pulled Westerman aside to advise him of it and gave orders that only he was to be aware of this; the crew were not to be told

The local agent, sent by Meldrum to check out the reason for the diversion, had been denied access to the aircraft on the grounds that it had been parked in the military compound due to space constraints. He eventually met Shaun in the briefing room, where the next plan was being prepared for the short hop to Dubai. Having got over his righteous indignation and been reassured that it was purely a security matter, he confirmed that Meldrum required them to operate through Dubai, collecting his party on the way, and then to proceed to Bahrain, where they could take a rest. However, they were to be on standby as there would probably be a further flight for them before they could be released.

Yes, thought Shaun, I bet there is, and I bet I know where it's too. He said nothing, leaning back over the counter to pull another flight plan form from the pad. May as well submit both here, that way they could get through Dubai as soon as possible.

Back at the aircraft, Jim, now in the left-hand seat, was going through the preflight checks for both of them. He had spoken to Pete of their misgivings, and the SAS major, more reticent than usual, agreed that whatever was planned, their future in the next couple of days was a little doubtful to say the least. Jim had gone as far as saying once again that a contingency plan was in place and that he and Longstop were welcome to tag along if they wanted to.

Westerman had muttered his thanks, said he would mention it to the sergeant, but that he thought they would see it through to the end. Pointedly, he did not ask for any detail, leaving the flight deck as the Digger returned from his external check.

'Okay, Jim, she is about as full as it's possible to be. I pumped until it came out of the surge tank vents and you can't get any more on than that. I would guess we have a good 15 hours, depending on how many take-offs we have to make. Anyway, we have enough to get us out of trouble, if we get the chance.'

'Good one, Dig, but I reckon what we will do is fill up at each stop. That way, no one will realise we are full because the amounts will be small. Our actual range will be our little secret, okay? Unless they check back this far, it's quite possible they will have us down for no more than a few hours and it might be quite useful to us for them to think that. When you have fixed up your panel nip, aft and ask Longstop if they managed to get any more out of that Thai fella. Seems to me we should know a bit more about what is being planned here. The authorities must have something up their sleeve. Pete is a bit quiet, maybe his opo will be more open.'

The Digger, checks completed, went to find Longstop, with whom he got on well. Actually getting the SAS sergeant to converse in sentences at all was no mean feat as all the others ever managed was a grunt, or at best one word.

It appeared that the Thai had given very little more information as to the final destination, other than that it was in Iraq somewhere. What he had said was that the cargo was to be paid for in gold and that it was to returned on the aircraft when it left there.

'And how much would that be, then?' The Digger managed to keep the rising excitement out of his voice, but only just.

'Well, his own share was to be US $1 million, but he seemed to think the whole deal was about $30 million.'

'Jesus, and we are going to bring that out with us, is that it?'

'Yep, looks that way. Of course, you don't know about it, do you?'

Digger managed a smile. 'Never heard a word, mate. What happened to the Thai bloke in the end?'

Longstop looked deadpan, 'He didn't make it. Probably food poisoning; you can't trust the chow in these Arab nicks, you know, Dig.'

'No, I guess not,' was all the Digger said.

Returning up the staircase, he sat in his seat. Shaun, in the right-hand seat, noticed the big grin. 'Jim! The Digger has heard something. God, will you look at the man? He's about to explode.'

Jim glanced over his shoulder. 'Okay, Dig, what have you got?'

There was silence as he completed the news, followed by a low whistle from Shaun. 'This could be our lucky day. Up to now, we have put everything on recycling the aircraft in the Cape Verdes, but this is a whole different ball game. You say we bring it out with us after the drop? Well, it's odds on they won't let us loose with all that dough without some sort of guard, and the so-called good guys are going to want to get their hands on it, too, if they can.'

They sat in silence for a while. Clearly, this new opportunity had a few strings attached.

As it turned out, the concern over the major's reticence proved to be unfounded. Having returned from another briefing session, he boarded the aircraft, called the flight deck on the internal phone and then asked Longstop, who was sitting in the front of the cabin, to close the door and then follow him upstairs.

When they were all together, he leaned forward over Jim's shoulder. 'That voice recorder system, Jim, it's not on at the moment, is it?'

'No, Pete, it comes on automatically when we start the engines, but we can switch the thing off even then if we want to. You think that's a good idea?'

'Well, yes. I want to go through a few things with you.'

Jim leaned back in his seat, located the required circuit-breaker and pulled it out. 'There you go, mate, now we can say what we like, even when we are on the move. What's on your mind?'

'I've just been told a whole bunch of stuff, most of which affects you boys. I've also been told to keep you in the dark. As I said right at the beginning of this, that's not my way, but I am going out on a limb here, okay?'

Nobody said a word.

'The Thai guy didn't make it, but before he left us, he let on with a little more detail than we got. It appears this stuff is destined for Iraq and they are going to pay for it in bullion; $30 million was the figure, and you guys are supposed to bring it out with you.'

He paused, but again nobody said a word. Hardly surprising as they already knew that much.

'The trouble is, the head shed are worried because the general feeling is that even the fruit loops in the North Korean government would not go for a bullion payment. Swiss bank transfer would be more secure even though it is traceable these days. Anyway, the feeling is that we may be dealing with a bunch of renegades, at least on the North Korean side. They also let on that this Gulf Arab imports company that's buying this thing is owned by a cousin of Osama Bin Laden. I guess you will have heard of him, eh! That has made them all a lot more nervous, if that were possible. Apparently, the Yanks have already seriously considered shooting us down. The Poms stopped them by coming up with this tracing business.'

'Thank Christ for the Poms,' muttered the Digger.

'Yeah, well, don't be too quick with the praise, Dig, because I was told just before I left that London, at the suggestion of the Yanks, ordered a radio-controlled device placed next to the centre wing tank bulkhead at the back of the forward hold. Apparently, it is not active at the moment. Like the ones in the guidance systems, it is switched on by satellite, with the added feature that they have wired it into the aircraft's power supply. With aircraft power on, its on standby, the satellite switches it on and then they will be able to trace the aircraft by satellite and destroy it whenever they want to, with the explosive charge attached to the receiver.'

'Bastards! What about us?'

'I don't think any of us figure very high in the stats here, Digger. The last thing they told me was that we should expect to be met in Bahrain by the people who are buying this thing, and that we can anticipate a quick trip to Iraq, probably Baghdad. They seem to feel we will be okay until we get back to Bahrain. From then, on the estimate of longevity on our part is not good.'

'And what about Meldrum and his mob? Are they going in with us?'

'Not known as yet, Shaun. Apparently, the people they have in Bahrain have tentative leads on the Koreans and they are still looking for the Iraqi connection. Again, the feeling is that while the Thai had indicated that Meldrum and his lot were to be paid off from the bullion, it may well be a different sort of metal, delivered quite a bit faster, if you get my drift! Not that he would be any loss. It appears he was being blackmailed into shipping drugs for the Thai cartel. That business in Curtin was the first shipment. It was after that went wrong the fix really went in. They got him filmed in Bangkok. Pretty unpleasant stuff, apparently; the bastard's a raving paedophile, they say. It also appears your mob is in dire straits. The usual suits have had their hand in the till. Word is, the company will be lucky to survive. Anyway, I've been told it would not be a problem if he didn't come back.'

'So, if I understand the situation, Pete,' Shaun began, 'we leave somewhere in Iraq with $30 million in bullion on-board after delivering the guidance systems. They are not going to let us out of the place with that on board without some form of security, are they? And you guys are coming in with us, is that it?'

'Yes, that's the plan. They feel they want us along through the whole deal now. We are to take care of any of their security ex-Iraq if necessary. As you say, they figure we will not come out alone.'

'Well,' Shaun continued, ' there's one problem we will have to fix up before Dubai, Pete, and that is the fact that Meldrum knows both of you from Curtin. If he sees either of you we are all done for.'

'Bloody hell, I had clean forgotten that!' He thought for a couple of minutes. 'Can Longstop and I move into that electronics bay after Dubai?'

'Well, yes. It won't be much fun; it gets a bit hot in there, but I guess it is the safest option. We should be able to get you off and on in Bahrain as crew after Meldrum and his lot have gone.' Shaun, glancing across at Jim, who nodded his agreement, turned in his seat. 'Pete, we need to talk some more about this. As you have probably already figured out, this is a one way trip for us. We've given you enough hints, I reckon, but this bullion thing could make a bit of a difference to our thinking.'

'Yeah, me and Longstop figured that out a while back. We will help you all we can, okay? I reckon a chunk of the loot may well find it's way into the MEC from the forward hold on the way back, say three million or so. Don't suppose they will miss it, and I figure you blokes will have earned it by then.'

'Thanks, Pete. Why don't you bung in a couple extra for you and Longstop, eh?'

'Might just do that,' Pete said. 'I guess we had better get this thing started, then.'

Jim glanced at Shaun, who keyed his mike. 'Seeb ground, Trans-Pac 101 for Dubai with info, Golf, start and push from the military apron.'

'Trans-Pac 101, cleared start and push, clearance is available when you're ready.'

While Shaun copied the airway's clearance, Jim and the Digger completed the after-start checklists. A final confirmation that the clearance was what was loaded into the inertial navigation system and with the push back tug disconnected they were ready.

'101, taxi,'

'101, Roger, straight ahead. Cross runway 26, taxi via delta and alpha, hold short and call ready on a 121.7.'

Shaun read it all back and Jim opened up the thrust levers to get the SP moving.

As they reached the holding point, the final before the take-off checklists were completed, again a nod from Jim was all that was needed.

'Seeb tower, Trans-Pac 101 ready.'

'101, Roger. Squawk 3251 runway heading to 2,000, then right turn direct to SADIR, climb to 5,000 and call departures. 119.3 cleared for take-off.'

Shaun flicked on the strobe lights, landing lights and transponder as he read the clearance back. He set 5,000 in the altitude select window as Jim lined up and opened up the thrust levers.

Digger's hand came up behind Jim's to fine-tune the take-off thrust setting as the SP accelerated rapidly through 80 knots. They all realised that the critical phase was fast approaching.

CHAPTER NINE

Crew bar, Gulf Hotel, Bahrain

She had been there an hour. It wasn't in her nature to wait. In the old days, it had been her that kept them waiting. However, this was hardly a date, more a summons, and anyway, it had given her time to reflect. No matter how she looked at it, she was 'in it' again.

Maria had been in the Gulf on and off for about two years now, After the dreadful business in Bangkok she had gone home to Mum, well, Dad really. She adored her old man. He never asked questions, but was always there when the tears flowed and they had flowed quite a lot in the months that followed.

It was from her mother that she got her looks, which where decidedly Latin. The irony was that it was her father who was from Spain, although, tall and fair-skinned as he was, no one would have guessed it.

She was never certain why she had become so emotionally fragile, eventually putting it down to the real fear of being put in jail by the Thais, in the days before Jim and the boys had got her out of the place. In the quiet moments of the night, she admitted that this had only been part of it, kicking herself for letting that man slip away. It had been very special and she doubted that 'it' would ever pass her way again.

After about six months of doing very little, she had woken up one morning knowing that today would be different. Not that she forgot the lessons; that would never happen. No, it was just a need to get back into the world.

She had first of all gone to an agency and done anything that came along. It wasn't long before people started to notice her, for not only was she quite strikingly beautiful, she was also very smart. The two law firms where she did some of her time each suggested a more permanent contract, although in one case she was reasonably sure the partner in question had a little more on his mind than legal briefs.

She turned them all down, still not ready to settle to one position. Finally, through a friend, she met the woman who was to be her boss for the next three years.

The company ran trade fairs all over the world, concentrating in the Persian Gulf and Europe. The fact that she was fluent in Arabic and French made her doubly valuable and before too long she was second only to the boss, trusted with running the whole show and loving it.

It was about a year ago that the new partner had joined. Her boss explained that she wanted to introduce some new blood and capital now, and as they did most of their work in the Gulf, it was natural that the partner should be from there.

Initial apprehension soon evaporated. The people at Gulf Arab Imports seemed very pleasant and she had to admit that nothing had changed at all, she still ran the place more or less single-handed. Only when she was in Bahrain or Dubai did she ever see them and the odd extra job that came up provided a welcome change from the normal routine, even if some of the tasks were a little strange.

It was about six months after the amalgamation that it happened. She had been at her desk, she remembered. The phone rang. Her mother very distressed, Dad in an ambulance, suspected heart attack, she should come home as soon as possible. She had dropped everything and got herself home in thirty minutes, picked up her mother and continued to the hospital. So began the longest night of her life. The old man had fought it to the end but the attack had been massive and the damage so great that even his formidable will eventually gave up. Devastated, they had returned home to look at the empty chair, the slippers; even the cat that had always sat with him in the evening knew, and had disappeared.

It was six months before she came to terms with the fact that he would no longer be there for her, although she always had the feeling that he was somewhere near. It gave her comfort.

It was probably her father's death more than anything that made her take the job when it was offered. The approach had been from Sheikh Anwar himself. He was obviously aware of her loss and, with the charm and consideration for which the Arabs are well known, she could hardly resist. Of course, it would mean more time in the Gulf, but the way things were that didn't seem to matter any more. She took the offer.

The new position was really no more than an extension of her old one; the only difference was that she spent more time involved in the Arabian end of the partnership, and that was more concerned with imports and exports than with the trade fairs. That being so, she was still responsible for the exhibitions in the area and it was at the most recent of these that this particular problem had surfaced.

It was, of course, her Arabic that had bought her here again and again. The locals had got used to having a female to deal with, but there was no doubt that being able to converse in their language made things much easier. This particular show was defence equipment and was due to last two weeks. However, the setting up phase was another two in front of that. Then she usually tacked a week on the end to lie in the sun and relax before heading back to the cold in London, unless something came up with the Gulf end of the job.

At least, that had been the plan until last week. She had to admit they had been bloody clever; the initial approach by the quite literally 'tall dark stranger' had been very smooth.

A chance conversation in the hotel lobby had led to an equally apparent chance meeting in the bar and dinner had followed. It was as they sat in her suite later, she in anticipation of what was to follow, that it had all come unravelled.

He had got her a drink and sat opposite her. He went on to explain that he needed her help with something, explaining that he worked for the government. Sitting there with her mouth open, she was so surprised she didn't even think to ask him which one. In the next half an hour or so he told her that they knew everything about her, who she worked for, and where. Their interest, he said, was in Gulf Arab Imports and she would be required to find out what she could about a few things.

Eventually, she recovered and exploded, telling him to get out and yelling that they couldn't make her do it.

He had let her rant and rave for a while and then pulled a package from his inside coat pocket. 'I suggest you settle down, Maria, and take a look at what's in there; it will change your mind, I'm sure.'

'Miss bloody Fernandez to you, you bastard! Christ, I was just getting the urge to hop in the sack with you, you creep, I really am losing my touch.'

However, curiosity is a powerful weakness and she bent to open the packet.

On top was a picture of her mother standing in the front garden with her Dad's beloved roses behind her. 'What's this, then?' she began. 'So you know where my mother lives; surely you're not threatening me with her?'

A sudden chill came over her.

'I am sure it won't come to that, Maria, we are just letting you know that we know. Now, carry on. You will find it all interesting, especially the stuff from Thailand.'

Now she was really frightened. That had been years ago and she could not believe that anyone was still interested. First there was a picture of her taken in Bangkok at that time. Scared as she was, she was pleased to see her figure had not changed much. It was a fleeting moment, for when she saw the next item, her blood ran cold. It was an arrest warrant issued by the Supreme Court in Thailand, with an accusation of large-scale smuggling, money laundering, suspicion of being involved in the movement of drugs and a fair bit else besides. If that was not bad enough, the final piece of paper was an Interpol warrant for the same list of allegations.

Looking at this last page, she realised that both warrants were dated 5 years ago. Christ, they have had these all that time and I didn't know. Totally destroyed, she eventually looked up and, close to tears, whispered, 'I didn't do anything down there. I didn't know. You must believe me. I was set up by my Syrian boss.'

'It doesn't really matter what we believe, Maria, it's really a question for the Thais and they quite obviously would like to talk to you. Even if you get off, and it's a big if, I don't think you would like the wait for trial in a Bangkok jail. Pretty lady like you, I reckon you'd be busy all night every night – for a while that is. Of course, you'd catch every exotic disease known. Way I hear it, they've got people in jail there with bugs that will kill AIDS, and you can bet they are all going to want to share them with you.'

That finished her. She started to weep, shivering with fear at the thought of it. Eventually regaining some of her composure, she managed to whisper, 'What do you want me to do?'

He had stayed another hour, calming her down, explaining that all that was really required was that she keep her ears and eyes open. They would have specific requests from time to time, but it would be nothing too dangerous. She was not to worry about the Thai business; He would sort that out for her. Finishing his drink he left.

That had been about a week ago, and since then she had heard nothing until last night. The call had been brief. Crew Bar in the Gulf hotel, 1900. No 'please', no 'thank you', just be there, and she was.

At 2005, he walked in, stood awhile looking, and seeing her, strolled slowly over. 'Sorry I'm late, Maria. Bit held up, I am afraid. Things have warmed up rather quickly in the last few hours and we have a job for you.'

'You bastard,' she seethed, 'I have been sitting here for an hour in this bar. Just about every one of these bloody pilots has had a go at me. Serve you bloody right if I had taken up one of the offers, wouldn't it. What job?'

'Best not talk about it here. I have organised dinner somewhere private. Can't afford to be seen together too much, you see; that's why I picked this place, no locals.'

She followed him out, aware, as always, of the eyes that followed her to the door.

'Well,' he began, as they sat in the private booth in the exclusive dining room on the roof of the hotel, 'you certainly turned the flyboys' heads. You could almost hear the sigh as you left. I guess they are all envious of me.'

'Yes, well, you have got no chance, mate, I would rather have it off with a rattlesnake. Come to think of it, it would be about the same thing, wouldn't it? Damn you.'

He smiled. 'Glad to see you are completely recovered. They said you were a tough one; I guess they were right.'

'Oh, yes, and who's the 'they', then? As if I didn't know,' she snapped.

While they ate, he told her what she had to do.

Her company had apparently purchased an aircraft, a Boeing 747 no less, which they wanted to know about. She was to find out what it was for and who was going to use it. They also needed to know where it was to be based and what special equipment it had on board. They were aware that it had been fitted out in Sydney, but as yet the actual details of what was on board were not available.

'Sydney, you say? And who did we buy it from?'

He glanced at his notes. 'A mob called Trans-Pacific, it says here.'

She only just managed to control herself. I wonder... it's just the sort of thing those three would get involved in. 'And when is this aircraft going to arrive, then?'

He looked at his watch, 'In about twelve hours, we think.'

'What! And you want me to get this when?'

He smiled, 'Well, yesterday would be good.'

She sat there shaking her head. How the devil was she going to do this? She had at least had one piece of luck, as about 7 days ago Sheikh Ahmed had mentioned that she would be required to arrange the onward sale of this very aircraft. At the time she had not thought anything of it; the company was, after all, buying and selling stuff all the time. She certainly hadn't gone into the details as yet. That was about to change.

'I'll get on to it tomorrow. As it's Friday, I may well be lucky and have the place to myself. Where can I contact you?' She purposely made no mention of the Trans-Pacific connection or the fact that she might well have access to some information already.

He pulled a card from his pocket and gave it to her, '24 hour watch on that, so any time is okay.'

She made no comment, just pushed back her chair and left deep in thought. I wonder…

The distance from Muscat to Dubai is only 183 nautical miles, so Shaun had planned it at a low Flight Level 200 (20,000 ft), the estimated flight time about 30 minutes, given that some manoeuvring would be required at the other end. The SP joined airway BA16 at position SADIR already climbing through 15,000 ft at 2,500 feet per minute, having accelerated to 320 knots.

Shaun turned round to Pete, who was sitting in the seat behind Jim. 'I guess you know all about that out on the left, don't you?'

The large massif behind the coastal plain was just visible in the moonlight.

'You mean Jebel Akdar, the Green Mountain? Sure do.

Bit before my time, of course. Were you down here then?'

'No, I arrived here just after that particular shindig, but the boys at Hereford told us all about it, secret then, of course.

These days everybody seems to know what happened there. I'm surprised that Spielberg bloke hasn't made a film about it yet, with the Yanks as the good guys, of course. I'm sure he thinks they won the bloody Battle of Hastings, you know!'

They all grinned.

Shaun was very Irish when it suited him, but he had firm views on who was allowed to take the piss out of the English, and Yanks were not very high on the list.

The battle for Green Mountain had been one of the first of the Special Air Services post-war success stories. It, plus the nasty little war further south in Dofa that followed it, set in concrete the fact that special forces had a permanent place in the British army. It was a measure of their formidable reputation that the concept had been copied by most of the First World armies, including Australia.

They began the descent at 60 miles out, completing the first of the series of checklists required. The dull roar of the engines at cruise power decreased to no more than a whisper, faintly heard, as the aircraft's nose dipped to the horizon. At 5,000 ft, Jim decelerated to about 240 knots and called for the first stages of flap. As the SP slipped through 3,000 ft, lining up on the localiser beam transmitted from the end of the easterly runway, the aircraft slowed a little more. The landing gear was lowered and the flaps were extended fully just as the glide slope beam gave its initial descent instruction. Jim increased thrust on the four great engines a little, to balance the extra drag, so that a dull rumble replaced the low-pitched whine of idle thrust, all that had been required until now.

All too soon the wheels brushed the runway, exactly 1,500 ft from the end, and reverse thrust, brakes, and the air brakes slowed them down to the walking pace that would enable them to turn off the runway to the allocated parking area.

'Bit different from Curtin, Jim.'

'Sure was, Dig, bit more concrete to play with as well. These Gulf airfields are never short of distance. I wish the rest of the world would get the idea; it would sure make our lives easier.'

They were told to taxi to a remote stand as their stay was to be short. Steps were sent out and the Digger went down to do his walk around check. On the way, he lifted the hatch to the MEC compartment so that Pete and Longstop could descend into their new home.

'If it gets too hot in there, I reckon you could move back into the forward hold until we get to Bahrain, but if you do that, make sure the inside curtain is secure before you come back into the MEC when we get there, okay? We don't want them to realise that we can access the place, do we?'

Pete looked up and smiled. 'You bet, Dig. Don't worry, it will all be like new. Just don't forget us, right?'

The Digger lowered the hatch, pulled the carpet back into place and made his way to the forward door, opening it as the stairs were being driven into place.

With the plan already filed, all the pilots had to do was to swap seats and begin the routine of checks required to start the whole process again. They were soon finished.

'When this is all over,' Shaun began, 'I think we will have to take some time off somewhere real quiet. Because if this goes the way it's supposed to, there are going to be some really pissed-off people who would like to speak to us, mate.'

'You had better believe it, Shaun. Still, with what we have set up, I reckon we can expect about $5 million each from the aircraft, at least that is what Miami Mike says. Then if we can ease a further three out of the hold after Baghdad or wherever, we should be able to live quite well for a while I reckon. It's a good thing you have connections over the water, mate. We can at least lie low there for a while.

'I've got to say, old Mike's idea of selling it back to the insurance company as salvage really makes me laugh. I'd like to be a fly on the wall when they make the call to tell the owners their shiny shag-wagon is on the ground on Sal Island. What's the betting the suits won't have a clue where it is?'

'No bet, Jim,' said Shaun laughing. 'Of course, before all that we have that little shit and his mates to put up with and I do believe they are about to arrive. Action stations.'

The limousine pulled right up to the door and Meldrum, the new chief pilot and the operations director got out, making their way to the stairs.

Eventually Meldrum himself arrived at the flight deck. 'Where the hell have you been?'

Jim slowly turned around, 'Morning, Mr Meldrum. Where we have been is Muscat, as you well know, and the reason we were in Muscat, Mr Meldrum, is because some dickhead sent us to an airfield in Thailand, where the fuel supply has probably not been checked since the Vietnam War. We had a double flame out and you could have easily lost the aircraft, but don't you worry, it's okay now and we're fine, thank you.' He slowly turned forward again. Meldrum, completely missing the tone, continued. 'And where is our Thai friend? I hope you haven't left him behind. I gave clear instructions that you were to bring him?'

This time it was Shaun who spoke, 'Why, do you mean he isn't here? He left the aircraft in Muscat. I don't think he had a lot of faith in your maintenance arrangements, said something about going with a proper airline. Nasty piece of work, if you ask me. You should watch yourself with that one, Mr Meldrum. Still, if he's not here he may have gone direct to Bahrain.'

'When I want your opinion, I'll ask for it, Fitzgerald,' Meldrum snapped, but clearly the news that the Thai was not on-board had worried him because he turned on his heel and, pulling the mobile out of his pocket, was dialling before he had reached the door.

Shaun started to laugh. 'Did you see his face? That has really got him worried. I wonder who the hell he is ringing?

CHAPTER TEN

Bahrain, Gulf Arab Imports

She had gone to the office early. Apart from the fact that it was cooler, it was Friday and it was unlikely that any of the staff would be there on the holy day it was even more unlikely that they would come at this hour. Sure enough the only person there was the security guard and she had found him asleep in the lobby of the building. After much embarrassment at being caught and pleading not to be reported, she had promised him that it would be their secret. After all, she had told him, she didn't really want people to know she had been there either.

She had found the file soon enough and reading it didn't tell her much, except they seemed to be paying an awful lot of money for an old aeroplane. There was an attachment that seemed to detail the avionics equipment that had been part of the package. It ran to about 30 pages of technical specifications, all of which were beyond her. The details on the future owner were clearer. It appeared that it was a large construction company in Riyadh. Something that did strike her as odd was that the sale price seemed to be exactly what they were paying for it; No profit for Gulf Arab at all and that was most unusual.

On a hunch, she pulled out a directory of companies in Saudi and looked up the new owners. She was immediately surprised to see listed as one of the directors Sheikh Anwar, her boss. Something else that caused her brow to furrow was the name of the CEO. At least it answered the 'no profit' question.

She sat and thought about what she had found. Obviously, this would be of interest to her 'new' employer, she thought, pulling a face·as the memory returned. The technical stuff seemed to be what they wanted, but then the details on the final owner or end user, a term she had become quite familiar with in the Bangkok days, would be sure to stir them up.

It was the Bangkok connection that decided her. When you have the information you at least have a degree of control. I'll not mention the technical stuff yet. The fact that I can show them where the thing is going and who the new owner is should keep them quiet for a while.

She went to the copy machine.

Trans-Pacific 101

The distance to Bahrain was just a little more than that from Muscat to Dubai. At 240 nautical miles or so, FL 200 was again all that was required. They joined the one-way airway system operated by United Arab Emirates control at a point about 40 miles out. Levelling off at 20,000 ft, they turned to join the west-bound airway, Mike 302, then onto Golf 462, before the final 40 miles from position PIMAL to Bahrain. The whole thing took about 40 minutes.

Meldrum had reappeared on the flight deck as they taxied in, telling them that he would be staying at the Ramada and they were to go to the Gulf hotel, where he would contact them when he had more information. As soon as they had parked, on a remote stand once more, a car had appeared and Meldrum, the operations director, and the chief pilot were driven away.

The driver, Shaun noticed, was Asian.

They waited a few minutes and then the Digger went down the stairs to open the hatch to release the two SAS men. As they surfaced, Pete said they had both moved back to the hold and had a sleep.

'Lucky you,' was all Digger said.

The two pilots joined them at the doorway, having completed the shutdown of the auxiliary power unit now that ground power was on the aircraft.

As they descended the stairs, two large trucks with UN on the side appeared on the right-hand side of the aircraft, stopping at the front and rear holds.

Jim wandered over to them, returning after a few minutes. 'They say they are from the UN relief agency and that they have been told to load the aircraft with food for Iraq. Well, it probably is food, looking at the sacks, but if those ugly-looking bastards work for the UN, I'll be very surprised. They were all armed as well; nothing too obvious, but they're tooled up. Now why would they need guns? I can only think they are here to make sure our special cargo doesn't go adrift. I told the bloke in charge to load it equally in the front and rear and that we will need to have a look in both before we leave. That stirred him up a bit.'

Digger was talking to the man from BP, telling him to fill it up. Roughly 45 tonnes should do it. These details taken care of, the five of them walked to the terminal for the inevitable document inspection. The processing was as cursory as usual and within minutes they were on the sidewalk organising two cabs for the Gulf hotel.

Within twenty minutes they were climbing out at the hotel, which was situated quite a bit out of town on a small peninsula of reclaimed land, on the road past one of the Emir's palaces.

The man who greeted them was surprised, as he recognised them. A broad smile replaced his usual scowl. 'Captain Fitzgerald and Captain Kennedy; sirs, it is good to see you again. It has been so long.'

'About three years I reckon, Hassan.' Shaun said, shaking his hand.

Just at that moment, Digger walked round the car and Hassan started again. 'And Mr Digger as well; this is a great day.'

The two SAS men were standing back watching. Neither could resist a smile themselves at the obvious affection this man had for the three airmen.

Jim explained after the handshaking was completed. 'We've known old Hassan here since we first started coming through Bahrain years ago. Then he was the bellboy under a lovely old gent we all called the Major. Word was, he had been a sergeant major in the Indian army during the war. He used to run this place as though he hadn't left it! Poor old Hassan here used to get some stick, didn't you, mate? Still, he was a great old boy. Taught you all about this job, I guess'.

'Oh, yes, sir, the major was quite a man to work for. He is still alive, I think; last I heard he was living in Karachi. He would have been very happy to see you all today, you know.'

'Hassan here is from Oman. We have just come over from there; place is certainly coming on. You been home lately?'

'Yes, captain, I was there one month ago. I have got another wife now,' he smiled.

'How many is that then, Hassan, you randy old bugger?'

'Only three, sahib. That is enough for any man, don't you think?'

'Three! Bloody hell, we haven't got one between us.'

They all laughed and went into the cool of the lobby, which had white marble walls and floor, ensuring that the desert heat was kept at bay, assisted by a large dose of air conditioning of course.

The formalities completed, Shaun strolled across to the Omani, who was busy instructing two young men as to their duties with the bags. 'Hassan, you still know pretty much what goes on round here?'

'Of course, captain. What is it you want to know?'

'Well, we are up here on something a bit different and we're a bit curious to know whether certain people are in town. We are particularly interested in any Koreans or Iraqis. They will be together, if I am not mistaken. Could well be over at the Ramada. Does your cousin still work out at the airport?'

'Yes, he is now head of security out there.'

'Great. Do you think he could keep an eye on our aircraft? It's the black one. You can't miss it. The thing is, there may be some unpleasant characters hanging around out there, so if he could let us know?'

'Of course, captain, it will be done.' With that he glanced sideways, and in a blast of Arabic told the two young bag boys that these men were special friends of Hassan, that they were to be looked after and that no tips were to be accepted.

'Grief, Hassan, you even sound just like the old major.' Laughing, Shaun followed the others to the lift to his room, so he could get some long overdue sleep.

Gulf Arab, The office

Maria had, on a whim, made two copies of the file on the purchase of the aircraft. It had taken no more than fifteen minutes but it seemed like an age. Pretty certain that no one would come in this early, she was still nervous. Collecting the papers, she inadvertently dropped the master file and, swearing hastily, shuffled it all together and returned to the office. There she put the master file back in order and returned it to the secure cabinet.

I don't know what I am so uptight about, she thought, I am supposed to be handling this anyway, aren't I? I suppose it's because I know what I am up to. Bloody good spy I'd make. Then she realised that that was exactly what she was and giggled quietly to herself. Placing one copy in the desk, she put the other in the briefcase and giving the office a last look, she walked to the door and left. The security guard was nowhere to be seen, which pleased her.

Once in the apartment, she dialled the number and was given her instructions by a voice she didn't recognise; certainly not her controller, she seemed to remember from some espionage book she had read that controller was the term used to describe the situation. She was to be in the crew bar at the Gulf hotel at 1900.

Perhaps it was the tie-in with the suggestion that she was being 'controlled' that got to her, for, having been given her orders, she snapped, 'Right, well, you can tell that bastard that I will be there when it suits me and I will wait for 15 minutes and then I am out of there, got that?' Slamming the phone down as she finished, suddenly she felt a lot better.

Having set up the rendezvous, she went back to the file and summarised the details of the sale of the aircraft with names, price and what appeared to be the place of final delivery. She added her own comments, pointing out the apparent incestuous relationship between Sheikh Anwar and the company in Riyadh. She made no mention of the technical data at all, suggesting that it must be in a different file and that more time would be required. Now with the afternoon to herself, she went to the pool that was part of the complex and lay in the shade, contemplating how this situation could be turned to her advantage.

Ramada hotel

Meldrum had only just got to the room in the Ramada when the phone rang. It was the Korean. He was summoned to another room and he was to come alone. Briefly cleaning himself up, he found the room and knocked on the door with considerably more confidence than he felt.

He was ushered in by a large Asian who said nothing, nodding to the lounge were Meldrum was to sit. About 5 minutes passed before the door of the adjoining room opened and the Korean entered, quickly striding across the room, extending his hand as Meldrum struggled to his feet.

'Mr Meldrum, my name is Lee Su Yung. I am a colleague of our mutual Thai partner. He has no doubt mentioned me to you?'

Meldrum, slightly taken back by the warmth of the welcome and the Korean's perfect English, murmured a rather inadequate, 'Pleased to meet you. Yes, he has.'

'I am becoming a little concerned over his whereabouts, Mr Meldrum. My requirements were that he was to be here to complete the Thai end of the business. As he has yet to be paid for his services, it is most unusual that he is not here.'

'My information,' Meldrum began, 'is that he positioned on the aircraft from Utaphao as planned. I mentioned to you from Dubai that there was a problem requiring a diversion to Muscat; something to do with the fuel system. Apparently two of the engines stopped. The crew told me that our Thai friend had been concerned about the delay the repairs had caused and had told them he and his men were going to take a regular flight directly to Bahrain. That was, apparently, the last they saw of him, but I took the precaution of having my local agent go to the airport. He confirmed that our Thai friend had already left. He also checked the scheduled departures and confirmed that there were four late bookings on the Gulf Air flight to Bahrain that left about 90 minutes after my aircraft arrived. I am afraid I can't tell you any more than that. Have you checked the arrivals?'

'Yes, we have, and it is most curious. The four reservations you mentioned were certainly made, but apparently there were coincidentally four no-shows. I think we must assume that either our Thai friend has decided to leave us or something more difficult has occurred. I think I will have to have a chat to your crew about this after they have delivered the cargo. They are to be disposed of anyway, as you know.

'However, the loss of our Thai friend is not a major problem. His part in this has almost been completed and what remains to be done can quite easily be managed by the two of us. There will, of course, be an increase in remuneration for you and your staff now that we seem to be somewhat reduced in number. It is perhaps time to give you more information on exactly what is in the hold of your aircraft that is so valuable to our clients.'

Meldrum, who had immediately responded to the suggestion of an increase in the fee, listened intently.

'You will obviously be aware that the cargo is diplomatically delicate, I am sure. There is no need for me to be too specific; it is enough that you realise that the so-called allies would be most upset if the nature of the cargo and its intended destination were to get out. It is a military shipment, which is why our Iraqi friends are so generous with the fee.'

'And may I ask just what sort of fee that would be?' Meldrum managed.

'Well, I think I can say that you and your colleagues will have the problem of disposing of, say, $5 million in bullion.'

Meldrum choked on the drink he had been given, much to the amusement of the Korean.

'I see you are impressed. There is, however, one more task I must ask of you to earn this fee.'

'And what would that be?'

'Actually, it is more of a courtesy to our clients really. We require a representative to accompany the shipment and accept the required payment on our behalf. A simple task that will involve no more than a short flight to Baghdad and back. I would think it would take about eight hours. A small effort for such a large fee, I think you will agree?'

Meldrum, aware of a feeling of unease, began, 'Surely one of your own people would be more suitable?'

'I agree Mr Meldrum, but there is a problem. I have no one of sufficient stature, other than yourself. I had originally considered our Thai friend for the task but his disappearance leaves me no alternative, as I am not in a position to go myself. I can assure you there will be no problem. The Iraqis are not the most pleasant people, of course, but we have been in business for a long time and they are not going to cause difficulties to one of their few friends. I want you to arrange for your crew to fly over there tomorrow, leaving at 1200.

They will have been told that it is a cargo of UN donated supplies and, in fact, a large quantity of food and medicine is being loaded as we speak.'

Special Intelligence Service (MI6) HQ, South Bank, London

Sir Robert Fraser sat, hands steepled, his substantial chin resting on them. He was deep in thought. Yes, everything seemed to be going well; the aircraft, now on the ground in Bahrain, was being loaded with the UN stores the Gulf Arab people were using as cover. His own staff had advised him of the heavy security presence that would have appeared a little over the top had they not known of the real cargo buried under the blankets and baby food. The only outstanding items were the procedure for the collection of the bullion when the aircraft returned, and the small matter of the crew and their new agent in Bahrain. He would arrange for the Bahrain authorities to monitor the progress of the gold until the Israeli strike, ensuring that it was not moved from the island.

As to the crew and the new agent, he thought the people at Gulf Arab would take care of that as soon as they realised what had happened. He would ensure that they had enough time to deal with that little problem before arranging their own elimination. The Americans will be pleased and the Australians as well. So be it; time to put the cousins across the water in the picture, then a quick call to Canberra to thank his opposite number there. Might even suggest a knighthood; that is, if it wasn't going to offend their sensibilities. These Antipodeans had become tiresomely touchy about these things of late, still he would offer it and see.

He was about to lift the phone to make a call to his Langley counterpart when there was a knock at the door. Irritated, he raised his head and growled, 'Come'. The woman who entered was a little ruffled he could see, and anticipating bad news, he nodded at the chair opposite. 'Well, what is it, Victoria?' he began.

Victoria Manning was head of the recently established department dealing with commercial exports that may be of an embarrassing nature. This had been formed after the revelations of the Iraqi weapons programme had surfaced. Its remit was to ensure that manufacturers of equipment that could be used in an offensive manner or for the production of weapons were controlled. Its staff routinely visited those companies involved. They were generally regarded as a pain in the arse by the commercial sector and cooperation was not always forthcoming.

Vicky, as she preferred to be called, began, 'I am afraid we may have a bit of a problem, Sir Robert.'

'Yes, I gathered that, young lady. What is it?'

'Well, it concerns that aircraft sale you are interested in at Bahrain, sir. I have just been made aware that it has some rather special equipment fitted that could cause us some embarrassment.'

Sir Robert, his attention now fully alerted, leaned forward, 'What sort of equipment?'

'Well, it's to do with the radar systems. Actually, we have been aware for some time that a small company in the Midlands has been developing a system that inhibits and then modifies the radar returns of targets fitted with this equipment. As you know, an interrogating radar pulse is reflected from the target, this is the primary return. To add to this, a system of secondary radar was developed whereby, on receiving the primary pulse, an on board transmitter sent a much stronger pulse back. This has been used for years in civil aviation and that secondary pulse has been routinely encrypted with information such as height call sign and speed, among other things.'

'Yes, yes, I am aware of all that. Get to the point, young lady, I haven't got all day.'

Blushing, she continued. 'Well, sir, it seems these people have developed a system which responds to the primary return, but with completely false information. Apparently, it can move the position of the aircraft some miles; it can also change its altitude and speed, in fact, just about everything. You can see that it will make interception just about impossible for aircraft and missiles, at least active homing missiles. I suppose infrared weapons will still work, but, of course, they rely on the interceptor knowing where the target is, anyway.'

'Surely the primary return will still be there, won't it?'

'Yes, it will, sir. Unfortunately, we have only just been made aware that this company has also developed a complete radar absorbing kit for the system as part of the package. It involves painting the aircraft with a radar absorbing compound, which is black. Apparently, this compound has the ability to reduce even a 747's signature considerably. As the false return pulse will overpower it, the feeling is that an interceptor's on-board computers will ignore the low-level returns and lock on to the false info.'

'And now you are going to tell me that the aircraft in Bahrain has this stuff fitted, right? And that it's painted black, yes?'

'Yes, I am afraid it has and it is, sir. It seems that there was a request for in-service trials and Trans-Pacific Airlines offered to fit it to an aircraft of theirs. None of the British airlines were willing to have one on the ground long enough to have the equipment fitted. It now appears that this aircraft was being reconfigured as a VIP transport anyway, so these Trans-Pac people lost nothing. It also appears that it has been sold on, to you know who, with the stuff still on-board. It is either incompetence or the Trans-pac people have pulled a fast one and used the fact that it has this capability to add to the sales package. I have to say, sir, that from what I have been able to find out about the airline management, I think it is probably the latter.

'Of course, it's only a prototype and there are apparently no technicians from the manufacturer on-board; the trouble is, we are advised that the stuff is really very easy to operate and it is possible that the crew may have figured it out. I have already initiated enquiries with the various air traffic control units along their route from Sydney to the Gulf to see if there were any unusual blank spots. All I have come up with at the moment is an unusual frequency change with the Darwin unit. The trouble is, the controller in question has gone fishing: walkabout, the locals call it. No one is sure where he is. The Australians have said they will try and locate him but they did not seem optimistic.'

'So, what you are telling me is that I have an aircraft which is about to go into Iraq fitted with a device which will make it all but invisible and loaded with a whole lot of stuff we would rather they did not have is that it?'

'Yes, that's about it, sir'

'Bloody brilliant, Vicky.

When this is over, there will be some changes. In the meantime, get on to the CEOs of these companies and tell them that we will be proffering charges. That should quieten them down. You can also find out why the hell an Australian airline is doing trials on UK defence equipment and how a bunch of civilians can sell the stuff to a company that is on the NATO watch list. Now get out, I have work to do.'

As the door, closed he let a sigh escape. Thank God he hadn't made the Langley call. Most embarrassing that would have been, as everything was quite clearly not under control. However, the situation was not nearly as bad as first appeared. He still had the ability to destroy the aircraft at any time and this, he reflected, really neutralised this new problem quite satisfactorily. Of course, he would have some housekeeping to do when it was all over, both externally and internally. Certainly the Antipodean knighthood was on hold.

He would just call Canberra to reassure himself that the two Australian SAS men were going into Iraq with the aircraft as previously arranged, and that the details for the return of it and the disposal of the bullion were as agreed. Although as Bahrain was part of the UK's area of influence, this was really only a courtesy, he would have been happier if the military element had been British. However, even that had an upside, in that if it all went wrong it would not be his people who disappeared. The fate of the crew did not concern him one bit.

CHAPTER ELEVEN

Crew bar, Gulf Hotel, 1800

This bar was for the exclusive use of airline staff and hidden down a corridor off the main lobby, it provided some relief from the hustle and noise of the main bar which, since the opening of the causeway, had become increasingly popular with Saudis escaping their teetotal regime. The problem was that as few of them were used to uninhibited access to alcohol, the effect was invariably noisy, and sometimes violent. The hotel had thoughtfully provided this alternative for the crews.

They had been there about a quarter of an hour. Shaun had spent a few minutes with Hassan, who had told him that his cousin had been unable to get too near the aircraft, as the Koreans had the area under continuous guard. He did say, however, that nobody had entered the aircraft and, as the stairs had been removed, it was unlikely that they would. These guards appeared not to be from a local company; the men were not Bahrainis. He thought they were Iraqi, but the one who appeared to be in charge was oriental.

Jim had been called by Meldrum in the late afternoon to tell them that they were to be available tomorrow for a short delivery flight of UN relief aid to Baghdad, departing at 1200, and that he would be accompanying them.

The conversation had then returned to the whereabouts of the Thai. Meldrum sought reassurance that the man had left the aircraft in Muscat with the intention of continuing to Bahrain. Jim had confirmed this. Putting the handset down, he had reflected that the loss of the Thai was obviously causing someone concern. Somehow, he didn't think it was Meldrum who was worried, although the fact that Meldrum and friends were to join them on the flight was perhaps something to do with it, as it was very unusual for their boss to get so near the dangerous end of anything.

The information of their unwelcome passengers caused some rearrangements, in that the two SAS men would once again have to travel in the MEC compartment. It was arranged that they would go out to the aircraft early to allow them time to do this.

The three of them sat in a quiet corner of the bar, awaiting the arrival of the SAS men, who had yet to make an appearance.

Pete and Longstop turned up after a few minutes and they ordered another round before settling into a discussion of tomorrow's activities. The news that they would have another uncomfortable ride did not seem to bother the SAS men. Pete, again demonstrating a flexible approach to the orders he had received from Canberra, but which, from their content, had obviously started life in London, told them of the latest developments.

'It seems, fellas, that the Brits have rumbled the fact that you have all that special gear on-board. I was told that your company was contracted to do trials on it for the manufacturer. It sounds just like your boss to go and sell it on before they get a chance to test it. You have got to laugh at the cheek of the bastard. Apparently the Poms are going nuts, going to keelhaul the manufacturer and if they ever get their hands on Meldrum, Christ knows what they will do to him. However, as he is up to his neck in this other business, they are sitting tight until it's all over. One thing that is a bit of a worry is that they have apparently already run a couple of tests on the comms in the bugs, including that one on-board with the self-destruct. It's a good job I didn't disable them before, but as they know about the secret stuff I'll disable it after we leave Baghdad, that way you will have the option of invisibility, if it all works, of course! I am right in thinking you three will not be around for long after we get back, yes?'

A nod from Shaun sufficed and Pete continued. 'We don't want to know the plan, but as I said, we will move some of the bullion forward to the MEC on the way over. It will be quite a while, if ever, before whoever ends up with the rest of it realises that some has gone for a walk. I figure you blokes have earned it, anyway. I guess this will be our last night together, so Longstop and I would like to buy you a few beers, or at least the Aussie government will. It's been fun working with you all. I hope we can do it again sometime.'

Jim spoke for them, 'Well, from our side, Pete, I think we all agree that if it hadn't been for you and Longstop, we would probably have bought it at Curtin, so we owe you two. I'll not go into the detail of the plan, but you're right, our intention is to let them unload the aircraft when we return and, as soon as the dust settles, we are going to refile for somewhere like Bombay and get the hell out of here. It will not be Bombay.

'We reckon, as we always have, that once this part is complete, whoever ends up running this show will want us out of the way, so we aren't going to stick around and find out how. The little bit extra in the MEC will help us for sure, and there will be plenty for you two when you want it. Just don't forget to disable that transmitter, will you? In fact, thinking ahead, perhaps it would be a good idea if you showed one of us how to do it and how to hook it up again without blowing ourselves all over the place. We have arranged to dispose of the old girl and it is highly likely that a reconnection later could take some of the heat off us.'

'Sure, no problem. We can do that in the morning before Meldrum and his mates arrive, okay?'

'Yeah, fine. If you two keep an eye on the news in the next few weeks, you will know where to find us.'

The SAS man looked at them and said nothing more, just gave a slight nod. It was enough.

It was Shaun who saw her first. Maria stood in the doorway, looking for her controller. Seeing the agent sitting in a booth on the opposite side of the room, she moved to join him. As usual, the conversation died as the men looked in admiration.

Jim, who could see nothing, started to turn. Had it not been for Shaun's lightning grab for his arm stopping him, he would have seen the cause of the sudden lull. Glancing up, he was surprised to see the frown on his friend's face as he slowly moved his head from side to side. A whispered 'wait' was all that was required to stop Jim from turning further.

'It's Maria, mate, but she is with somebody that Hassan pointed out to me earlier as trouble, reckons he is government or something. I figure we had better find out what she is up to before you go barrelling over. You know what she is for getting into trouble an all'.

Jim swallowed. 'I'll get Hassan to find out where she is living and then we can have a quiet chat.'

They were relieved when after a few minutes Maria and the man she had joined got up and left. She had not seen them.

As the door closed behind them, Jim let out a great sigh. 'Thanks, Shaun. Good job you stopped me. I would have reacted for sure. How did she look? It's been a few years, I guess?'

'Stunning as ever, old son. You would have done something dumb for sure.'

Pete, who like the rest of the bar had stopped and looked, glanced at the three of them. 'Well, that's the lucky lady from Bangkok, eh? I can see why you would help her out. You are a lucky guy, Jim.'

Jim, embarrassed, could manage no more than a smile.

The rest of the evening was spent sorting out the detail of their departure and how the Baghdad end of things should be handled now that they were aware, from the call earlier in the evening, that Meldrum and his two cronies were along for the ride. It meant, of course, that at least there was someone on the inside who could deal with the Iraqis. That could be useful because it took the spotlight off them.

Jim, with his mind on other things, did not take much part in the rest of the conversation. After about an hour, the two SAS men made their excuses and left.

Shaun looked across at his friend and said to the Digger, 'Dig, see if you can round up old Hassan, will you? Ask him to come in for a chat.'

Digger pushed his chair back and left.

'You okay, old son? I can see it's hit you a bit hard.'

'Yeah, I guess so. It's just a bit of a shock after all this time and it's all come rushing back, you know how it is.'

'Thing is, Jim, I suspected she was here. Hassan spoke to me earlier about her. He doesn't know who she is, of course, but he described her and I half suspected. Irish intuition, I guess. The trouble is, he seems to think she may already be involved. I asked him to poke around a bit so we will see what he has come up with before we do anything more.' Even as he spoke, he could see that his old friend was not really taking it in. They sat in silence waiting for the Digger to return.

She and her controller had returned to the rooftop restaurant where she, determined to milk this for all it was worth, had refused to give him anything at all until she had worked through the most expensive parts of a very expensive menu. Only at the point of coffee did she pass over the file on the dealings of Gulf Arab imports, aircraft purchase and the names of the company's principals. She was a little disappointed with the reaction she got. It amounted to little more than a grunt; only the name of the Riyadh director seemed to cause any interest and even that was muted.

He looked up, 'And this is it? I thought I told you we wanted all the details on this business. There is nothing here on the actual aircraft at all. We happen to know that it has been fitted out with some special equipment and I do not believe you would not have come across some reference to it. Not holding out on me, are you, Maria? Because if you are, it will only take a quick call to the Thai embassy. It's only about a mile away, you know.'

Try as she might, the beginnings of a blush flushed through her face. Only the low light and her quick temper saved her. 'You prick,' she hissed, 'you tell me to get what I can and when I do, all you can say is it's not enough. Well, stuff you. There is another file but it was with my boss and I do not have access to it. The only reason I know it exists is that it is referred to in those notes you have there. You would have seen that for yourself if you had read them properly, instead of having a go at me.'

Even the agent leaned back as the full force of her venom washed over him. 'Just checking, Maria. It's good as far as it goes. Trouble is, a lot of it is known to us. What we really do need is details of a Korean and an Iraqi connection; also the stuff I mentioned on the aircraft and we need it as soon as possible. Tomorrow would be good.'

She all but choked on her coffee at that. 'So because you already know about that, it's my fault, is it? You really are a prize wanker, aren't you? I get the stuff you want at considerable risk to myself, and now you decide you don't need it. If you are typical of British intelligence we are in real trouble.'

Smarting from this, because he had to agree she was right, it took all his powers of persuasion and a good deal of flattery mixed with an occasional veiled threat to get her to try again first thing tomorrow.

In the taxi on the way back to her apartment, she reflected on the intuition that had caused her to hold back on the technical information. It was obviously a trump card. The Korean/Iraqi thing was going to be more difficult as, so far, she had seen no reference to either.

As the vehicle stopped outside her block, she saw four men standing there; one the tall Omani she recognised from the hotel. At first she was not sure, but it was the Digger, or rather the Digger's shape, that made her realise that yet another piece of the past had returned.

Ramada Hotel

Meldrum sat in the suite he had in the Ramada and glared at his two subordinates. He had just given them the good news of their imminent little trip to Baghdad, with predictable reactions.

'I do not see why it is necessary for me to go,' began the new chief pilot in the irritating falsetto that already had Meldrum gritting his teeth.

'I don't bloody well care what either of you think. The Koreans have control of the money here and it has been made very clear to me that if I want to see that money, and I would remind both of you, that also means you, we will see this through to the end. I am not going into this alone, so make up your minds.'

Needless to say, after the usual grumbling, they both followed the cash and agreed.

'Right! We will leave at 1200 tomorrow. It's about a one-hour flight I reckon, about three hours on the ground to unload the UN stores and the special cargo and then load up the bullion, and then we are away. We should be back here by 2000 at the latest. The Koreans will arrange the removal of the bullion. Then all that remains is for us to confirm the agreed Swiss deposits for the sale of the aircraft with Gulf Arab, the transport cost of whatever it was we bought here, plus the bonus for tomorrow's little extra business from the Koreans and we are out of here. Why, we even pick up a little extra as we will not have to pay the bloody crew! The people at Gulf Arab have agreed to deal with that little inconvenience. They are going to offer them a contract to fly the aircraft in to Saudi, Riyadh, I think. Naturally, once they are there, they will disappear. I am going to tell them that we will settle with them after they return. I must say that getting rid of those three will give me a lot of satisfaction.'

Fernandez Apartment

They had gone to her apartment and talked for some hours. The information exchange was revealing to them all. The fact that the authorities were aware of the special equipment but did not seem to be fully aware of its potential, confirmed by the request for more information from Maria, was a little confusing. Why could they not get this from the manufacturer?

It was Jim who figured it out. 'I bet they don't know how good it is because the trials were incomplete. In fact, they may not even have started. I reckon the manufacturer is unable to say what it will do for sure. So it's my guess we have a system about which these people know very little, and that could be very useful.'

For her part, as the sheer delight at seeing them all again subsided, she could see that, in fact, she had told her controller nothing that he did not already know. The technical file she had held on to would have been much more use. This evening's meeting, ensuring that it would never be handed over to her controller.

They all agreed that London would be quick to get the information from the makers. Their only real advantage was that it appeared that they were the only ones who were aware just how effective the stuff was. That, and the knowledge that just because London knew, did not mean that the information would be available at the pointed end of things, at least not at first. They spoke at length on the escape plan in general terms, not wishing to give out too much specific detail. Maria had confided that she was being blackmailed.

Shaun had asked her to find out the one piece of information that had eluded them so far, which was the name of the Arab insurance company that was covering the aircraft and details of the policy if she could. Maria had said this would not be a problem. In fact, she could probably find the telephone number of the CEO if they liked.

Shaun had thought for a while. 'You know, that could be very useful, particularly the CEO bit. Yes, I like that. Can you get it before we leave tomorrow?'

'Of course, but how do I get it to you?'

Jim scribbled the numbers on a piece of paper. 'We are planning on leaving at about 1200 tomorrow, so a call here before 0930 should be okay. If not, there is the mobile but it is not as secure.' Jim then asked her what she intended to do when the aircraft returned.

'I wasn't going to do anything. As far as I can see, they will lose interest in me as soon as you three disappear,' she paused 'Am I missing something here?'

'Well,' Jim continued, 'don't know about the others, but for my money, when this thing breaks I reckon anybody associated with it is going to be fair game. We have already had it made very clear that, as far as the establishment is concerned, we are expendable, so I reckon that even if they leave you alone, the baddies will want blood. I think you should plan on leaving this place tomorrow afternoon. Take a break in the UK. Thinking about it, it would probably be best to lose yourself until the heat dies down; you will see what I mean in a few days. In the meantime, I reckon it would be best to get a flight to Paris or Rome, and then make your way to the UK overland, assuming that's where you want to go. Oh, and when you get there, keep away from known friends or relatives. The Brit intelligence people are not on our side in this; don't forget that.'

Seeing that Jim wanted to talk to her some more, Shaun stood indicating to Hassan, who had sat in silence while his friends discussed their future. They moved to the kitchen followed by the Digger, Shaun leaned toward the Omani and whispered, 'Hassan, old mate, the girl could be in real danger here and we are not going to be in a position to do much this time. Any chance you can arrange a bit of protection? At least until she gets out, we can cover any expenses. It may take a little while, but you will not be out of pocket.'

Hassan smiled, shaking his head. 'Captain Shaun, sahib, it will be a pleasure, and no payment is required. I will speak to my cousin at the airport. We will have people here within the hour. She will be guarded until she leaves.'

Shaun, as always touched by the genuine affection this man had for them, smiled. 'You're a good friend, and when this is all over, you will not be forgotten, I promise you. Now, we have a long day tomorrow. I think we will have to drag Jim away. God knows when we will sleep again, or where.' He moved back into the lounge, coughing as he did so, giving them time to at least gather some composure. 'Guess we should hit the road, Jim, we need some sleep, old buddy.'

Jim nodded.

The brightness of her eyes showed how close to tears Maria was. 'Must you go, Jim? Its been so long and...' her words faltered.

'Look, love, we have to get this done. Once it's all over, I will be in touch, okay? You just make sure you take Shaun's advice and get the hell out of here.' Reluctantly he got to his feet and walked to the door. The others moved in front giving them a few precious moments.

Hassan opened the doors of the car and within minutes they were away. The journey to the Gulf Hotel passed in silence.

Maria had woken early, even for her; she wanted to be in the office by 0600. She noticed the tall Omani standing across the road. A slight wave of the hand had been enough to tell her that Hassan had been true to his word. As she pulled away from the kerb, she saw him sliding into a nondescript car to follow. At the tall office block she entered her dedicated spot and the Omani parked opposite, moving to the front of the building as she gathered her bag to follow him.

Early as she was, Sheikh Anwar was earlier, greeting her as she closed the inner office door, causing her to jump in surprise.

Damn, she thought, I needed some time alone in here now it's going to be bloody difficult.

'Come in here, Maria, I have work for you.'

God already, what can he possibly want this early? The boys weren't due to leave for a few hours yet, so it can't be them, and I had hoped to organise a flight out before anybody arrived, let alone the boss. She smoothed her dress down, quickly checked herself in the mirror. Not bad for 0600, she thought. 'What is it you want, sir? You are in very early this morning.'

'Yes, it is a most important day,' he began. 'We have our aircraft on a special charter to Baghdad and the return cargo is of great interest to us. However, I have just been informed by the Iraqis that they are not going to complete the deal in one day and they wish us to organise a second load of UN supplies for tomorrow, when the balance of our return cargo will be loaded. This is most inconvenient and typical of these people. If the contract were not so lucrative, I would not do business with them. As it is, our Korean partners will be most upset at the delay as they were planning on leaving us tonight. This will mean that they will delay their departure until tomorrow.' The tone indicated to her that this was not something Sheikh Anwar looked forward to.

'I want you to contact the UN people and suggest another load as the aircraft is required to return to Baghdad. Offer the same rates as before. I would imagine they will be interested as they are always short of capacity and at least it will pay the fuel bill. Arrange the stores to be at the airfield early tomorrow morning.

'Will you also advise Mr Meldrum of this development when he returns from the flight today. He is at the Ramada.

He can then organise the crew. It will mean that the final delivery flight these people are required for will now be put back a day. You had better suggest to him that they are offered an increase in their fee for the extra flight. That should keep them quiet and then we can be done with them, once we have the aircraft in Riyadh.'

This first mention of the Korean connection excited her, providing as it did the chance to ask a question. 'These Koreans, sir, do you wish me to handle that?'

'Yes, perhaps it would be better coming from you. Impress upon them that the fault lies entirely with Baghdad and that they should direct any enquiries to them.'

'Of course. Er, I will need the file, sir, I have no record of the Korean gentlemen.'

'Oh, yes, of course, here,' he handed Maria the file.

She could not believe her luck. Clearly, the boss was distracted and if she was right, this file had all the information she was required to get. Now if she could only hold on to it long enough to copy it.

She made notes of the Koreans' names and their hotel rooms and the relevant telephone numbers, deciding that it would be a good idea to delay the call a little, at least until the aircraft had left; 1300 should do it. Her controller would be most interested in this development she was sure. A quick glance through the file confirmed that it was exactly what he was after. She heard the door of the main office close and, reaching for the intercom, she called Anwar. There was no reply. Moving to her own internal door, she confirmed that he had left the office. It took no more than five minutes to copy the entire file and return the master to her boss's desk. So far, so good.

A scan of the airline web sites got her a flight at 2100 that night, and a call to Hassan confirmed that he would collect her from the flat. Now all that remained was to get this stuff to the Gulf hotel and her controller. She would do that at lunchtime after calling the Koreans.

Opening her purse, she unfolded the number and quickly dialled. The Digger answered but quickly handed it across to Jim who, tearing the top page off the pad, wrote the required details on it. He was a little surprised at the name of the CEO. They spoke for a few more minutes, agreeing a future meeting, and then he slowly replaced the handset.

Without a word, he passed the note to Shaun, who glanced at the details, focusing on the name. 'Jesus, this is getting interesting.'

CHAPTER 12

The Airfield

With a departure time planned for 1200 local, there was ample time to sort out the details of what was going to be a long day.

The Digger was meticulous in his pre-flight, ensuring that once again the small amount of fuel required would not attract the attention of any interested party. He figured there would be quite a few of those. The guards looked on with bored disinterest, but he made a point of keeping well clear of the forward hold; no sense upsetting them. While this was going on, Jim and the two SAS men, suitably attired in an airline shirt and trousers, boarded the aircraft.

It was essential that they be on-board well before the arrival of Meldrum and his cronies, because the hatch was, of course, in the luxurious forward section and it was highly unlikely that the three of them would sit anywhere else. However, for now Longstop moved into the galley to 'get the billy on'. They had all indicated a cup of coffee would be welcome.

Pete Westerman had slipped down into the MEC to stow their weapons, and a couple of mattresses he had managed to inherit from somewhere. Jim had started to enquire where they had come from, but Pete just put his finger to his lips, saying nothing. Somehow Jim figured the hotel would be a couple short today. Just how they had got them out remained a mystery, but he would have bet that the hand of Hassan was in there somewhere.

Shaun spent the next hour at the briefing office. As a UN sponsored flight, it would have a UN call sign, United Nations Seven Zero Alpha in this case. The route was a simple run-up the Gulf, turning north to Baghdad as they crossed the coast just south of Basra. The UN official sent to supervise dispatch told Shaun that the aircraft would be met and unloaded by the Iraqis, the UN presence there being very small since the weapons inspection fiasco a few years ago. He said that as the cargo was blankets, medicine, and some food, there would be no trouble. Little does he know, thought Shaun.

At just under 400 miles, the flight would take about an hour. Shaun estimated a fuel burn of about 35 tonnes for the return journey, so a top up would be required when they got back before the next part began. He was careful to show an endurance of this, plus 60 minutes holding fuel, on the plan. Any subsequent inspection would show the aircraft as having just over the mandatory reserve fuel when it returned. The uplift of an estimated 35 tonnes would cause no real concern… at first.

While he was finalising the plan, Meldrum and the chief pilot arrived, leaving the operations director sitting in the car.

Meldrum began, 'Now, Captain, this is a very important operation, so I do not want any of the usual cock-ups, is that clear? I am going to have the chief pilot here check everything, and when we arrive I don't expect to see any of you three off the aircraft. There will doubtless be a ceremony for us and you are to stay on the flight deck while it takes place.' Turning to the diminutive chief pilot, he said, 'Can't have the hired help interfering in ceremony, can we? I want you to go over the plan and confirm it is satisfactory, and then join us at the aircraft. I will just check with the new owners that we are clear to go.' With that he turned and left.

Shaun, who had not said a word or even indicated that he was aware of their presence, moved sideways along the counter, pushing the plan in front of his new boss and said, 'Well, there you go, you little prick, see if you can find my deliberate mistake. If that arsehole thinks we are so unreliable, why doesn't he get you to fly the bloody thing? I'm sure Jim and the Dig would rather stop here, and I know I would.'

The chief pilot started to splutter. 'You can't talk to me like that...' stopping when he realised that there was very little he could do, under the circumstances. He passed a cursory glance at the plan turned and scuttled off.

Shaun, with a grin on his face, filed the plan. Boy, was he going to enjoy this. Pity none of them would be around to see the chaos when they found out their aircraft had been borrowed. Don't suppose anyone has ever nicked a 747 before. Should create one hell of a stir, he mused.

The clerk programmed the plan into the system. He gave it no more than a glance. The UN flights were a regular occurrence these days. It took no more than a few minutes to process the details and now, as long as they followed the plan, the authorities on both sides of the Gulf should be happy. A bit different to the reaction they could expect in a few hours, Shaun thought.

Leaving the office under the terminal building, he strolled out to the aircraft where Digger was just completing the external preflight check. He waited for him at the bottom of the steps, 'All okay, Dig?'

'Yep, she should get us there, wherever there is, of course. How much gas are we going to need on the return?'

'Well, I reckon about 35 tonnes all-up for the round trip, so it will only be a small load, nothing to attract their attention when we move out. They will have to trace the fuel loads all the way back to Muscat before they realise just how far we can go in this thing, and by then, with luck, we will be way beyond.'

'Let's hope so, mate. Personally, I'll be glad when this bit's over.'

'You and me both, Dig, so we may as well get on with it, eh?' Shaun moved to climb the stairs. The Digger followed, as always taking a last look around as he did so.

At the top, the two SAS men waited. Longstop, with the hatch to the MEC pulled open, was shoving the second of the mattresses down the hole while Pete stood drinking the last of the coffee.

'Looks like you two are going to be nice and cosy down there. We will keep it as cool as possible for you. I guess you had better get down now; I saw our illustrious passengers over at the terminal and I reckon they will be over shortly.'

Without a word, they climbed down the ladder to what was to be their home for the next few hours. The Digger slowly lowered the hatch, pulling the carpet back in place and generally tidying the area up. By the time he had finished there was no sign that it existed.

Shaun had gone ahead to the flight deck where Jim, whose leg it was to be, had completed the cockpit checks for both seats and was now sitting in the left looking into the distance. 'All done, Jim. The Dig's just putting Pete and Longstop away and once he's ready and the three stooges arrive we can go.'

As the engineer sat down and started his long series of internal checks, Shaun told them what had been said at planning. 'You should have seen the little prick's face when I said we were quite prepared to let him do it. I've never seen him move so fast. In some ways it's a shame we will never know how this turns out. Either way, it's certainly going to be a mess.'

The limousine that Shaun had seen drive off with their three passengers eventually reappeared at the bottom of the stairs and Meldrum and the other two got out, accompanied by an Asian man. They shook hands and then moved to climb the stairs to the door at door left one.

Jim told the Digger to go down and check that the door was secure once they were on board. He returned in a few minutes with the news that the three of them were sitting in the forward cabin, already drinking the champagne which had been loaded on the express orders of Meldrum. 'I wonder if the bastards would feel so bloody comfortable if they knew who was sitting in the compartment below them.' he said.

Checks completed, Jim turned and nodded at Shaun.

'Bahrain ground, United Nations 70 Alpha, start clearance, and standing by for ATC.'

There was a brief pause and back through their headsets the controller issued the airways clearance. 'United Nations 70A cleared to Baghdad via airways Golf 795, Bravo55, Basra, Alpha 57, Hashimiya. Climb to and maintain Flight Level 280 and squawk 5512. Cleared to start, call the tower on 118.5 when ready to taxi.'

As the clearance was issued, Shaun had checked it against what was loaded in the aircraft's navigation computers and set 28,000 ft in the altitude select window. The code of 5512 was dialled into the transponder. Now the various en route air traffic control agencies would be able to identify them.

As this was completed, Jim glanced round at the Digger who gave a thumbs up. 'Start 3.'

Within a matter of minutes, the four great engines were running, the after-start checks completed and Shaun had the taxi clearance from the tower. The long taxi to the runway end was taken, with the pre-takeoff checks completed as they approached the holding point. Shaun got their take-off clearance.

'Okay, guys, a rolling start and standard abort procedures. Let's go.' With that Jim slowly moved the thrust levers up to the vertical position and the Digger's hand came up behind as Jim applied take-off thrust. The Digger's job here was to fine-tune the thrust so it was symmetrical, as Jim was concentrating on the take-off.

The landing gear was raised and the flaps, so necessary for a take-off, had been retracted as the aircraft accelerated to its climb speed of 340 knots. Levelling off at FL280, they relaxed a little.

This was only going to last a little while, but for the few minutes they had in the cruise the three of them sat and marvelled at the effect of the searing glare of the desert sun. It made the line between the light blue of the Gulf waters and the horizon difficult to discern.

'Looks like we have company,' Shaun, glancing over his shoulder, had picked up the fighter. 'Have a look out your side, Jim.'

Jim looked over his shoulder, 'Yep, there's another one there, looks like a Tornado to me, which means it's the Royal Air Force. They must be keeping an eye on us, although I would have thought the return trip would have been their main concern. Maybe they are checking to see if we are on to the special gear? At least they won't be as trigger-happy as the Yanks.'

'My guess is they will follow us to the edge of the Iraqi airspace and use us to test the Iraqi radar. They will be wanting to see if the ragheads light us up, and if so where the radar stations are.'

Jim glanced sideways at Shaun. 'You know, old mate, once a bloody soldier, always a soldier. I wouldn't have thought of that, but you're probably right.'

The fighters peeled off as they approached a position called TAMIM, which was on the old border between Kuwait and Iraq. They could have come further as the no-fly zone covered all of southern Iraq, but Shaun reckoned the early withdrawal was so they could sit back from the border and monitor the Iraqi radar from a distance. As it was, he cleared with Kuwait centre and was passed to Basra radar. The guttural voice of the Iraqi controller came through the headset, confirming their route and clearing them to descend, when ready, to an initial altitude of 10,000 ft.

As it was, their descent did not begin until about 90 miles out, or some 30 miles before the powerful airway beacon at Hashimiya, by which time they had been handed over to the final sector controller at Baghdad itself. This equally surly controller cleared them to further descend to 5,000 ft and to contact the approach controller at the Saddam Hussein airport. Within a few minutes the approach sequence began as Jim called for flaps and landing gear. The landing itself was, as always, something of an anticlimax for them. Jim allowed the old aircraft to slowly decelerate to a safe taxi speed and turned off the runway. The 'follow me' car was already rolling as they manoeuvred to fall in behind it.

They were brought to a halt in an area where a large gathering of troops were on parade. The aircraft was stopped precisely so that the front door was in line with a blood red carpet. Clearly, the locals had this down as a special occasion. Still, given what was in the hold, none of them were that surprised. After all, a little pomp and ceremony would distract any prying eyes from the real business of the day.

The Digger, having completed his checks, left the flight deck to open the door. The steps were just positioning as he slowly moved the door open, only to be pushed aside as Meldrum forced himself into the doorway.

Even Meldrum was a little taken aback. A full guard of honour was lined up adjacent to the bottom of the stairs and a colonel in full dress uniform stood waiting at the foot, smiling broadly and holding out his hand in greeting. Meldrum's initial concern was quickly evaporating in the obvious glow of his celebrity status, although had he done any research on the perfidious Iraqi hospitality, he may have still been a little more concerned. As always, his ego allowed him to put any misgivings behind him and bask in the attention.

The colonel moved to greet him, warmly shaking his hand while smiling at his two colleagues who had descended behind him. 'Welcome, Mr Meldrum. Truly it is a great honour that you have chosen to escort the valuable cargo to us. My name is Colonel Sulliman from the President's Republican Guard. You are to come with me. The President himself wishes to meet you in person, to thank you for the effort you have made on our behalf.'

Meldrum, somewhat overcome, mumbled his thanks and then realised that this was not going to be something that was going to be over in a few minutes, as he had planned. 'I have one question, Colonel. My aircraft was to return with the, er, payment, to Bahrain as soon as it was loaded. Do I assume you will wish it to be delayed?'

A frown, quickly suppressed, passed over the Iraqis face, 'Ah! Mr Meldrum, I am sorry, but there has been a small change in the plan. Clearly, you were not informed by our Korean partners; very remiss of them. We are sending the aircraft back as soon as half the bullion is loaded, for another shipment of the so-called aid the accursed UN sends us. In the meantime, you will be our guest and much has been arranged for your entertainment.'

As the reality of this sunk in, Meldrum and his two associates began to feel distinctly uncomfortable. Furthermore, it became obvious why the Korean had been reluctant to accompany the cargo.

'May I just return to the aircraft for a moment to brief my crew, or at least have my chief pilot here do so? After all, they are expecting us to accompany them and they were planned to deliver the aircraft to its new owners in Riyadh as soon as they were unloaded in Bahrain, and there is the security aspect to consider,' he finished lamely.

'That will not be necessary, Mr Meldrum. As we speak, they are being briefed and the valuable cargo is being removed. They will be accompanied by four of my most reliable men on the flight there and back, so you do not need to concern yourself with security. Assuming all is well with the cargo, you will be on your way home tomorrow a wealthy man. Now, if we can all move to the cars, please, my President is waiting and he is not a patient man.'

With increasing alarm, the three were ushered towards a line of Mercedes limousines at the end of the red carpet, the irony of its colour lost on them.

CHAPTER THIRTEEN

Jim watched as Meldrum and the other two were fussed over by the Iraqis. He could sense that Meldrum was loving it, clearly in his element as they were eased towards the waiting cars. As he watched, though, the body language changed and Meldrum stopped and looked back with alarm on his face. Clearly something had been said that had caused him concern.

'Hey, boys, looks like somebody's just walked over the little shit's grave; he has obviously been told something he didn't like.' The other two moved to the left side windows to see Meldrum, the chief pilot and the operations director being gently but firmly ushered into the vehicles.

There was a quiet but firm knock on the flight deck door. The Digger moved to open it to reveal a diminutive official standing there.

He looked around and moved inside. 'Good afternoon. I am Sadik Ismael, from the Iraqi Ministry of Aviation. There has been a small change of plan,' he began.

Continuing, he told them that the return cargo would be shipped in two parts, the second depending on satisfaction with the shipment just received. Their new orders were to fly back to Bahrain with the first part and collect another load of UN relief aid. During this time, their superiors would be 'entertained' by the President and would be returning with them the next day. 'All being well,' was the somewhat ominous conclusion to this little speech.

'I am also to advise you that we will be placing four of our most trusted men on board for the round trip, to assist you with any 'difficulties'. You understand? We anticipate the cargo exchange will be complete in about 2 hours and then you will be free to go. Our men will be here within the hour and until that time I must ask you not to leave the aircraft, for your own safety. You will be aware that our people are a little angry at the current situation and some may well react in a, shall we say, spontaneous manner, in the sight of Westerners.'

Shaun spoke for them. 'No problem, my man. However, we will need to move around inside the aircraft and before we depart, our engineers will require to check the aircraft over from the outside, that's essential, so we will expect you to arrange that. Is that clear?'

The Iraqi, somewhat taken aback by the tone, being more used to those he considered underlings muttering simpering compliance, found himself agreeing as Shaun's unblinking stare held him.

Okay, you may go now,' Shaun said, completing the demolition of the Iraqi's ego.

As the man scuttled out, the other two burst into fits of laughter.

'Shaun, you are an absolute bastard, you know. Did you see the guy's face? So now we know why Meldrum and his mates were looking so worried.' Jim managed to get out eventually. 'I think that what we have got to do as soon as possible, and before this lot figure we are three, is get our two mates out of the hole. As Meldrum and friends are not coming back, there is no need to keep them locked up and we may need them up here if these four locals turn out to be what I think they are.'

They made their way to the main deck. The forward left-hand door was open and an Iraqi soldier stood at the bottom of the stairs, glancing up as the Digger stood in the doorway. While he stood there, the other two pulled the carpet aside and opened the hatch, moving back to allow the two SAS men to climb out.

'How was it?' Jim asked.

'Been in worse places,' Longstop rumbled.

'Yeah, I expect you have. Must have been like a hotel down there.'

Shaun spent the next 5 minutes filling the two of them in on the latest developments. In the ensuing discussion, the three airmen agreed that there would be no return trip; each considered it too risky. However, the fact that the Koreans in Bahrain would be anxious to get their hands on the second part of the bullion and would, therefore, make sure the second load of supplies were to hand, could work in their favour.

Pete began, 'I guess they will load half the gold. That should be about 15 mill. Still plenty to go around and the Koreans will just assume the balance is to come on the second flight; they won't realise that part of it is missing at first. Yep, I think it's all going according to plan. We will stay topside, as you suggest. We will have to take out these four jokers on the way over. Can't have them expecting to go back and you lot going off into the wide blue, can we? Even they would smell a rat after a couple of hours. No, I think Longstop and I have another little job to do. What about disposal? You could take them on with you, I suppose, but there is always the risk someone may find them in the transit, and stiffs always cause problems. Can't ditch them overboard, can we?

The three airmen looked at each other and Shaun said, 'Well, there is a procedure where we can open main deck doors in flight. It's part of the smoke removal operation. Can't say I have ever done it. In fact, I am not sure anybody has, but it's in the book so I guess it will work, and I reckon the door would open far enough to slip them out. What do you think, Dig?'

'Yeah, I reckon it would work. Of course, it will mean depressurising, but I reckon if we descended early into Bahrain we could cruise along at 10,000 ft for a while and slip them over the side. It's all water out there and it will be just on dusk. Assuming we de-identify them, some lucky prawn fisherman is going to get the best catch ever if they are in the water for a few days,' the Digger laughed.

'Bloody hell, Dig, and you think we're rough. That's put me off prawns,' muttered Longstop.

Checking that the forward hold was closed, the two SAS men and the Digger re-entered the MEC and from there the hold, through the internal hatch, where they showed the Digger the relatively simple process of arming and disarming the remaining tracker. Pete also showed him the way in which the tracker was hooked up to the self-destruct device and demonstrated how that in turn could also be neutralised. The device had been wired into the aircraft electrical system and, so as long as the ship was shut down electrically, the tracker, and through it the destruct device, were inert.

As the three men pulled themselves back through the MEC hatch, two vehicles pulled up at the base of the steps. From the back of the truck three soldiers, dressed in the black of the Republican Guard, jumped out, moving to the stairs, following an officer similarly dressed, who had arrived in the other vehicle, a jeep-like thing of Russian or Chinese origin.

The four men climbed the stairs and entered the aircraft.

The officer paused in the doorway, eyes adjusting to the light. 'Major Haddad,' he announced. 'I and my men here are from the President's Republican Guard,' he began. If he had expected a significant reaction to that announcement he was bitterly disappointed, as the five men sitting in the first-class area studiously ignored him.

Finally, Shaun slowly lowered the newspaper he was pretending to read. 'That's nice, you must be very proud,' he said, lowering his eyes to resume reading.

Clearing his throat, Haddad continued. 'We will be returning on the aircraft to Bahrain with you as a security measure and, until we are ready to depart, you are all confined to this cabin. Is that clear?'

Again, a few seconds were allowed to elapse until Jim removed his long legs from the back of the seat in front, unravelled himself in slow motion and, moving in a deliberate way, positioned himself in front of the Iraqi officer. 'And you, Major, would be well advised to ask before you enter my aircraft. We, too, are very security conscious, as you can see.'

A brief glance at the other four draped about the cabin in various degrees of anything but caused Haddad to scowl, but he said nothing as Jim continued.

'As we advised your civilian colleague, before departure our flight engineers here will require to do an outside inspection, and that, Major, is not negotiable.'

Haddad, regaining some of his composure, eventually managed to confirm that this would be allowed.

The loading was soon undertaken and the Digger completed his walk around accompanied by Longstop who, wanting to get a look around outside, had told the Iraqi that he, too, was an engineer and that the inspection was best done by two. As it was, the area had been cleared and the guards moved back to the hard stand in front of the nearest hangar which, incidentally, still showed the results of attention received in the recent war, in that the roof and rear wall were both missing.

Returning to the flight deck, the Digger began his preflight checks as Jim, now in the right seat, called the tower for their clearance, which was simply the reverse of that which they had used to get here. Having anticipated this, it was already loaded into the three inertial navigation computers. The four engines were once again started, in the order 3, 4, 2, 1, and as the clearance was received Shaun slowly moved out onto the taxiway leading to the duty runway. They had completed the preflight checklists as they reached the holding point. Take off clearance was soon given and the old SP turned into wind and began its take-off roll.

As it lifted off, climbing into the southern sky, Meldrum and his two minions stood on the spacious balcony of one of the smallest of Saddam Hussein's palaces on the banks of the Tigris. It faced south and they had a clear view of the aircraft's departure and, in spite of the warmth of their reception, and the attentiveness of their hosts, each felt a vague feeling of unease. They were now completely in the hands of these people, at least for the next 24 hours and, not for the first time, Meldrum cursed himself for not finding out what this damned cargo was. As it was, the colonel, whose job it was to see that their every wish was complied with, had told them that the President would be requiring their attendance shortly; in fact, just as soon as a sample of the cargo had been inspected. In the meantime, they were to eat and drink their fill and 'entertainment' would be provided as soon as they were ready.

MI6 London

Sir Robert sat once again at his desk, this time awaiting the appearance of the head of the department dealing with this matter. Things were, as far as he knew, going according to plan although, so far, the information from the woman in the Gulf Arab office had been disappointing, but, as the local agent had been at pains to point out, this was probably not her fault. She could not have known that most of what she had told them was already known. He had been assured that she would be going back to find the technical information they required. A knock on the door indicated that Victoria had arrived.

Dressed in a light green suit, the skirt set at her knees, she was very conscious of the glance at her legs from Sir Robert as she sat down. Pulling the chair towards her side of the desk, she began her briefing.

'It seems we may have the possibility of a small problem, Sir Robert. The agent we have in Gulf Arab has just contacted our man out there. She has come up trumps with the information we asked for on the Korean end of it. We have names, hotels, and even room numbers and Middle East desk is arranging round-the-clock surveillance and doing a check on just who these people are. They are also in the process of setting up the snatch teams for later.

'However, the other bit is not so good; it seems the Iraqis are going to pay the Koreans in two parts. She didn't say much, but she has been told to arrange for a second shipment of UN supplies to be bought forward to tomorrow. The aircraft will be used to deliver this as well, and then bring the second load of bullion back. She was told to advise their Asian friends of that. It would seem that the Iraqis are running checks on the system before handing over all the bullion. Apparently, the news was not well received. She said the matter was taken out of her hands pretty quickly. This Anwar individual, who we have down as the CEO of Gulf Arab, eventually ended up talking to the Koreans. Her opinion is that there has been a falling out between them.'

'And where does this leave us, then, Victoria?'

'Well, sir, we have had to put our Bahrain people on hold, gold-wise, and we can't really leak the girl and the flight crew to Gulf Arab until the rest of it has arrived. We may also have a problem with the Israelis. As you know, they have aircraft on standby to go in once these guidance systems reach the destinations. They are not going to be easy to stop once the satellite shows all the systems are static. Of course, if we forget the second shipment, it doesn't matter, but you were quite specific about us picking up all the gold if possible.'

'So we can either let the Israelis loose as soon as movement ceases, or delay until the aircraft has made a second round trip, is that it? And, of course, our cousins are going to tell Tel Aviv as soon as movement ceases, anyway, aren't they?'

'That's about it, sir. I don't know how much influence you have there, but if they go in as soon as the stuff arrives, I think we can say goodbye to the second half. I would guess that will be 15 million dollars.'

He paused, staring at the ceiling for a minute. 'Um, that is a lot of money for a few hours more, isn't it? I will talk to their ambassador and suggest a small delay in the strike. One can but try.'

'There is one other thing, sir. It appears that the CEO of Trans-Pacific, this Meldrum person, has gone into Iraq with two of his staff. Can't think why he would do that, but if what we have heard so far is anything to go by, the chances are there is money involved.'

'That could be useful,' Sir Robert said. 'We will need to make sure that character is dealt with at the end of this, anyway, and what better way than have the Iraqis do it for us? Shouldn't be too hard to fix up some uncertainty in Baghdad. Of course, if they are still there when the Israelis do their little bit of housekeeping, old Saddam will probably fix them up anyway, don't you think?'

'Yes, I think it would not be a good place to be,' she said.

'Now, as a matter of interest, just where are these guidance thingies at the moment?'

'Well, again it's starting to get difficult, sir; all but two have been static for the last hour. One of those is actually in Baghdad and it's our opinion that this is the one being looked at to satisfy the Iraqis that the stuff actually works, as I said. However, it is now moving slowly towards a local facility we know about. The second is the problem in that it is still moving west towards the Jordanian border. Of course, it is quite possible that this is more than one system. We have no way of telling whether the signal is from one or more transponders when they are loaded close together. This last lot are at least moving quite slowly, so it's road transport, which is a relief, as the others all appear to have been moved by air, but it is pretty clear the target for these last ones is going to be Israel.'

As she was speaking, she spread a large-scale map of Iraq on the desk. A number of red crosses marked current locations, with a blue arrow indicating the progress of the last shipment, presently three quarters of the way to the Jordanian border on the main road to Amman.

'Cheeky buggers, aren't they, sending the stuff down the main road? What's all this up north here?'

Victoria glanced down.

'Yes, you can see the pattern, sir. Northwest corner to take out the American base at Incerlick, Northeast, Teheran, Southwest the base at Tabuk in Saudi and then Southeast for the Gulf area. It seems that we have badly underestimated the number of missiles they have, Sir Robert.'

'Given that the last one is still moving and it is pretty clear this is the one that will most interest the Israelis, I may be able to negotiate a 24 hour delay. Can't say it's the money, of course. I will have to think of something else; concern for agents on the ground, something like that.'

The irony of that statement was not lost on Victoria, for in all the time she had known him, Sir Robert had never shown any concern for anyone but himself. The well-being of field agents were never a consideration unless their loss could be seen as a threat to his upward movement in the system.

He leaned forward and pressed the intercom. 'Get me Saul Leibeman at the Israeli embassy – now!' He never said thank you to those he considered underlings. 'So, Victoria, keep me posted on that last shipment and tell our man in Bahrain that I want some heat put on that wretched woman we have in there. I want more information on the state of the systems on the aircraft, and also more on the Korean end of this. The cousins have not been very forthcoming in that area.'

A wave of the hand and she was dismissed.

As the door shut, the call to the Israeli embassy came through. 'Ah, my dear chap, Sir Robert here. I need to have a chat with you about the schedule for the little piece of business we discussed. Your place or mine, old man?'

The negotiations began.

Baghdad

The banquet had been lavish, the food magnificent, served as it was by a bevy of beautiful women, most of whom, it seemed, came from the West. There were a couple of exceptions, the chief pilot noticed: the two pretty young men who spent most of their time hovering around Meldrum. Clearly, someone had done their homework. Meldrum was, of course, in his element, licking his lips in anticipation. But in spite of the sheer luxury and extravagance of their situation, the chief pilot was a worried man. There was, as far as he could see, no way out of this if the Iraqis turned nasty. He would be glad when the aircraft returned and got them back to Bahrain.

The colonel entered the room, smiling. 'Gentlemen, I hope everything is to your satisfaction. I must ask you to break off for a while; my President wishes to see you now, to thank you on behalf of the people of Iraq, in their struggle against the West. Will you follow me, please?'

The audience was brief. Saddam Hussein had thanked them, saying that he was pleased to inform them that the cargo was entirely satisfactory and that they would be well rewarded, without mentioning a specific figure. What most interested Meldrum was the suggestion that further business was available in the future and that, given the success of this, it would be lucrative. They would have been entirely happy with this if throughout they had not been aware of Udai, the President's now-crippled son, who had sat at his father's right hand, saying nothing, but looking on as a reptile might view a potential meal.

As it was, the chief pilot voiced his misgivings to Meldrum and the director of operations as they returned to the banquet room. Meldrum dismissed it, anticipating the evening's entertainment, but the operations director shared his concern. Neither could see a way out if it all went wrong, although at this stage all seemed well.

As they re-entered the room, each was met by two of the women and gently eased into a private room, each except Meldrum, of course, whose escorts were the two androgynous young men who had administered to his every need at the banquet.

They had been in the cruise for about 10 minutes now. The two Tornados that had picked them up as they cleared Iraqi airspace had given them no more than a cursory look, waggled wings and dived away into the gathering darkness below.

Pete indicated with his head to Longstop that it was time. As he left he said, 'Probably best if you lock this after us. Should be okay, but you never know.'

Digger got up to do it.

They went down the staircase, Longstop turning into the galley and Pete moving into the cabin and using the same procedure as before, asking if any of them wanted a drink. Unfortunately, on this occasion, all four declined, presenting the two SAS men with something of a dilemma. It was quite likely that without the element of surprise, one of the Iraqis may be able to retaliate, particularly as they seemed considerably more alert than the Thai thugs had been.

A briefly whispered conversation in the galley and Longstop moved through the cabin, towards the rear of the aircraft. After a few minutes, the internal phone at the forward door, adjacent to the seat in which the Iraqi major sat, sounded its calling chime.

Pete, moving across, answered it and after a few words he turned to the major, saying that his colleague had a problem in the rear galley moving one of the food containers and asking if he could get one of his men to help.

It's a funny thing about human nature; if a request is made of someone and they are out of their element, there is a strong possibility that they will comply. So it proved to be in this case, for without querying as to why the SAS man himself could not help, he turned and ordered one of his men to the rear. As the man walked aft, Pete returned to the galley and called the rear galley on the phone there. As soon as the line was open, he busied himself in the forward area such that the major could see him, keeping his attention.

The man ordered aft turned into the rear galley to be confronted with Longstop's back as he knelt on the floor. He moved forward and tapped Longstop on the shoulder and the SAS sergeant slowly turned, looking up. Only then did the soldier see the silenced Sig pistol in the SAS man's left hand. The soft 'phut' sound as Longstop squeezed the trigger was completely overwhelmed by the noise of the rushing air outside.

The slow-moving bullet entered the Iraqi's head underneath his jaw, tumbling as it struck the flesh of his throat. Converting the contents of his head to a mass of jelly, it hit the rear of the skull, was turned without penetration to finally come to rest at the base of the cerebellum, by which time life had ceased.

Longstop, already moving, eased the body to the floor, then glanced quickly up the aisle. No mess, no reaction; so far, so good, he thought.

Sliding the Sig into his waistband, he picked up the handset and muttered, 'One down.'

Each of them replaced their handsets and Pete again busied himself in the galley, fiddling with a box of circuit-breakers, which he hoped controlled nothing serious. Longstop began a slow walk up the left-hand aisle. As he reached the class divider, Pete moved out of the galley and, speaking as loud as was reasonable, asked again if anybody wanted coffee. With their full attention on Pete, neither of the soldiers was aware of the danger behind. In fact, both were down; each with a single bullet in the back of the head before Pete had taken out the Iraqi major.

'Piece of piss,' rumbled the SAS sergeant. 'Now comes the interesting bit: getting the bodies over the side.'

Pete picked up the handset again and dialled the PP buttons on the handset that gave direct access to the flight deck. The Digger answered and told them the door was open. They both returned there to discuss the next phase. As they entered, Shaun was already calling Kuwait centre, requesting a descent to Flight Level 100, the 10,000 ft altitude required to open the doors. The clearance was given without comment and the aircraft's nose dipped to the horizon as the descent began. Engines a dull rumble at the idle thrust, that was all that was required. In the 5 minutes or so that it took, they reviewed the long checklist associated with the smoke removal procedure that eventually required two doors to be opened. Only the last part was relevant, requiring the aircraft to be depressurised before the doors could be cracked.

As the thrust came up, the aircraft levelled at the new altitude; the speed was allowed to bleed to 220 knots, the slowest they could be without using the flaps.

An inquiry from Kuwait radar as to the reason for the early descent and slow speed was deftly fielded by Shaun, who concocted a story of a possible pressurisation problem, ending with the assurance that operations were normal and that they would continue at this level to Bahrain.

Digger and the two SAS men returned to the main deck to begin the grisly task. The Digger rotated the handle at the left forward door, having first deactivated the slide. The door in the now unpressurised aircraft moved inwards. The noise level was considerable. Moving aft he proceeded to do the same at door number four, the rearmost one on the SP, only this time he placed a restraining strap over the handle top to control the degree to which this door would move. It was through here that the bodies were to be passed, and as such it would have to actually be swung part open, whereas the forward door was barely cracked and re-pressurisation would force it home again.

Whilst he was doing this, the two SAS men stripped the bodies and pulled them to the rear, leaving them in the aisle. A quick inspection of the clothing revealed nothing of interest other than the weapons, Russian made Makarov 9mm automatics. These were placed to one side.

As the last body was dropped in the aisle (it was that of the major), Digger called the flight deck, telling Jim that they were ready to drop. The lower altitude and the few minutes all this had taken meant that they were now in complete darkness.

Jim gave the go ahead. One by one, the bodies were slipped over the side, again the major last to go. As the last one disappeared into the darkness, the Digger pushed the door to the central position and rotated the large handle. Forcing it home, he then did the same at the front, and immediately the noise level returned to normal and conversation was possible.

The Digger returned to the flight deck, leaving the SAS men to pull back the carpet in the forward cabin, lowering themselves into the MEC and through the internal hatch to the forward hold.

Longstop stayed by the hatch as Pete inspected the pile of boxes stowed in low crates on the floor of the hold. Piece of cake this, he thought, grunting as he lifted the first box, finding, as everybody did who handled gold for the first time, that it was much heavier than expected. He had already figured that there were about 500 bars there, and if this was half the 30 million that made each bar worth about $30,000, so a hundred of the them would be about right. Convenient, too, because it meant just removing the top layer. Between them, it took about 30 minutes to move the bars the few feet to the MEC area, where it was stacked around what amounted to the aircraft's brain.

Neither said much as they climbed back through the hatch and up the staircase, although Pete thought he heard Longstop at the back muttering something about 'bloody prawns being off'. Not for the first time, Pete reflected that his sergeant was a great bloke to have on your side, but he did seem to focus on the strangest things at times.

The approach and landing followed the familiar pattern and they were soon directed to park in the same area from which they had departed. Each noticed the expected reception committee. As the aircraft stopped, the engines slowly running down, the stairs were already being pushed up to the front door. At the right-hand side, the forward hold was being opened.

Longstop had already descended to the main deck and disarmed the slide at the front door. Pulling the handle forward, he pushed the door open. The two men standing there, one Arab, the other Asian, moved to board but paused as the SAS sergeant asked who they were in a tone that required an answer.

Sheikh Anwar introduced himself and the Korean, stating that there had been a change of plan.

Longstop motioned them to the staircase and followed them up. Entering the flight deck, Sheikh Anwar again introduced himself and his Korean colleague. 'I am afraid, gentlemen, I must ask one more task of you,' he began.

Jim in the right-hand seat turned sideways and interrupted. 'Yep, we know; the Iraqis told us you want a second run tomorrow. Is that it? Meldrum and the other two are still in Baghdad. Some sort of celebration we were told.' He continued, 'Right now, though, once your people have unloaded your cargo, whatever it is, we are going to secure the aircraft and go to the hotel for the night, right.'

The sheikh, unfazed by the news, continued. 'Good, so there is no problem. You will, of course, be paid for the extra flight, bringing the rest of our freight and your CEO and his colleagues out. We can understand our Iraqi friends wished to thank them for the assistance your company has given.'

'Yep, something like that. Now, if you can leave us, we still have some work to do here.'

'Of course,' Anwar said, and with a slight bow, turned and left.

It took the Korean's men no more than 30 minutes to offload the gold, last seen slowly moving to the main gate, escorted by a large car front and back, each filled with some tough-looking Asians. Even before the hold was closed, the fuel bowser had been connected and 40 tonnes of Avtur pumped in. Such a small load would bring no suspicion as it was sufficient for only about 4 hours, or 2,000 miles, and after they left there would be confusion as to their range. As it was, the aircraft was full to the maximum, giving a range of just over 15 hours, or about 8,000 miles.

The final job was for Pete to disable the tracker in the forward hold. This done and as the area grew quiet, the five of them gathered on the main deck.

'I guess this is it then,' Pete said.

Shaun, held out his hand to the SAS major, ' Yes, we'd better get out of here; we need the night for as long as possible and we don't want to be here if they check with Baghdad about the gold, or the guards, do we? I've just got a couple of calls to make on the mobile, and then we are off.'

The SAS major nodded at Longstop, who, moving forward, held out the two silenced Sig pistols 'I've cleaned them up and they have a full mag; each, there is more ammo in the box. I reckon you blokes know how to use them. Anyway, take care. It's been fun.'

That was about as much as any of them had heard from the SAS sergeant ever. Even Pete seemed surprised.

Each shook hands, mumbling their thanks, a little embarrassed, as is always the way with these men. Jim's final request concerned Maria. Pete agreed to check that she had got out of the place. Shaun moved away slightly and punched a long series of numbers into the mobile; a few brief words, another call, then he moved to climb the stairs, raising his hand as the two SAS men disappeared into the night.

'Wonder if we will ever see those guys again?' said Digger.

'I wouldn't doubt it, mate.' Jim said over his shoulder as they climbed.

'Sure hope so. I got used to having them around you know.'

'Yeah, me, too,' from Jim, as he entered the flight deck.

They had arranged for Hassan to meet them, so their departure was delayed a little. They waited, as the airfield had quietened down. Jim called Hassan on the mobile, to be told that Maria had been seen safely on the early evening Gulf Air flight to Paris and that he and his cousin would be coming out to the aircraft in about ten minutes.

The two Omanis entered the flight deck and quickly briefed the crew on what had happened during the day. Apart from Maria's visit to her controller and the ensuing flurry of activity, all seemed to be going according to plan. The Koreans and the executives of Gulf Arab were, they said, under continuous surveillance, but there was no undue interest evident in the whereabouts of the three of them. There being nothing further, they took their leave with a firm promise that, as soon as the dust had settled, contact would be made. Digger closed the door and Hassan and his cousin removed the stairs and, with a wave to the flight deck, moved off into the darkness.

'Another couple of good men we owe,'

Shaun agreed. 'Right, fellas, best we get out of here. I'll file over the radio, Bombay okay?'

'Sounds good to me, Dig. You all set back there?'

'Yep, ready when you are. Let's go.'

CHAPTER FOURTEEN

The departure had been made without fuss and as soon as they reached the cruise at 35,000 ft, Shaun had left his seat to return to the upper deck area behind the flight deck. Here he began the process of turning on the equipment they would need if they were to disappear. Jim, monitoring the on board navigation computers which were steering the aircraft along the airway system en route for Bombay, was also handling the procedural radio calls with the ground stations. The aircraft was handed over from Emirates control in Dubai to the last VHF facility at Muscat, on frequency 124.55. Jim called Shaun on the interphone circuit to tell him that they would be over position SULAR in a few minutes, with the boundary at MAROB about 25 minutes after that.

As MAROB approached, Jim switched off the transponder and the TCAS collision avoidance system. Whilst this meant that they were effectively blind to other aircraft in the vicinity, it also meant that other aircraft would have no indication of their presence. Finally he reached up, flicking off the switch for the navigation lights and the aircraft disappeared.

The expected call from Muscat centre, requesting the recycling of their transponder as contact had been lost by the ground, was not long in coming. Jim had replied that the second unit would be selected. He made no move to do so. At the same time, Shaun activated the on board equipment, which corrupted the aircraft position should a primary radar interrogate and lock on to the aircraft. With the increasingly urgent enquiries from Muscat centre in their headsets, they dropped out of VHF coverage and disappeared.

They maintained the track for about 50 miles and then, slipping down to 34,000 ft, Jim turned the old SP off the airway onto a heading of 180 degrees. It was their intention to hold this heading until about 15 degrees north latitude, and then head 220 to cross the coast of Africa, well to the south of the powerful radar at Aden and the French base at Djibouti. From there, it would be 270 degrees, right across the southern Sahara.

CIA, Langley, Virginia

The head of the UK desk knocked on the director's door. 'Just had the head of MI6 on the phone, sir,' he began. 'It's this rogue SP business. The latest seems to be that it's all going well, although there has been a last minute change to the schedule.'

The director, who had been deeply engrossed in a report on the increasingly difficult situation in the Taiwan Strait, where the Chicoms and the Nats were having another go at each other, looked up, remembering that the Brits were, to all intents and purposes, running this one. 'Oh, what sort of a delay?'

'Well, Sir Robert's people are telling him that the Iraqis have only sent half the bullion over and that they are holding the Australian owner and a couple of his people as hostages, pending an inspection of the goods. As yet, we haven't heard anything else on that end. However, from the satellite traces, all except one seem to either have arrived at or be on their way to a location. We figure that they are looking at that one, as it is currently static in Baghdad. The others are probably in the process of being matched to the missiles, all, that is, except one batch, which at the last check was still moving towards the Jordanian border. The Brits reckon this is the one that will set the Israelis off, as the targets are pretty obviously their back yard. Thing is, they have been on to Tel Aviv as well. They have asked them to hold off with the strikes until the aircraft has returned from a second trip to Baghdad which has been scheduled for tomorrow. Something about his people on the ground needing time to get out. Must say, it doesn't sound like him; my feeling is he wants to get his hands on the second load of bullion. We have also had a three-way with him and Tel Aviv. The Israelis have reluctantly agreed up to the point the last consignment stops moving. From then on, they want to start the mission. Apparently, everything is set. They have two KC135s on five minutes with two squadrons of F15s to follow. They are using a screen of F16s exercising on the eastern border and these aircraft will also provide cover for the bombers on their return. Total mission time is reckoned to be about two hours for the aircraft tasked with the sites on the Iranian border, less for all the others, of course. Naturally, none of this happens until we say so, because the final target data comes from us.'

'And we have all the proof we need about these things, do we? I need to be able to tell the President that he can go to the UN with absolutely no doubt about this because the "Fit is really going to hit the shan" over this.'

'Sir, we have the evidence from Muscat, the bullion, and we will have the people in Bahrain. The Brits are going to pick up the Koreans as soon as the news of the raid gets out, and the Gulf Arab people, once they have done a bit of 'housekeeping' for them. They reckon that the ab dabs will want to terminate the crew, the owners, and the inside agent they have there. Once that's done, they will pick them up.'

'Okay, so where are we right now?'

'Well, sir, the aircraft is on the ground in Bahrain. The crew will be resting. Another load of UN junk is being provided for the next flight. I guess this Anwar character figures we would be fooled by it and grateful. ETD is apparently 1000 tomorrow local; say eight hours' time.'

The phone rang on the director's desk. Picking it up without a word, he listened, the knuckles tightening, such that the skin was white as he replaced the receiver. 'It seems all may not be as well as you thought,' he began. 'We have just had a report from our man out there that a black 747 SP took off some time ago, and the filed destination is not Baghdad, it's Bombay.'

'What?'

'Yep, I reckon you had better get down there and find out just what the hell is going on. Don't forget that the aircraft and what's in it is what started all this, and I don't want it out there running around loose. Find out where that carrier is; *Nimitz*, isn't it? Put them on alert now. What's the range of this thing? Find out what the fuel load was. Chances are, it's not going to Bombay. Oh, and find out who is flying it. It may not be the Aussie crew. If it is, get me everything we know about them. Jesus, the damned thing could be going anywhere. Russia, China... Wait a minute, we have a trace on it, don't we? That should make interception easy. I am going to call the President and get an authority to destroy. How long is it from Bahrain to Bombay?'

'I'd guess about 4 hours, sir, perhaps more.'

'Okay, get to it. Assume you have the clearance, and tell *Nimitz* that the aircraft is to be intercepted and escorted to Muscat. Give them all we know about this special gear and that if the thing refuses, it is to be destroyed, got it?'

The deputy got up to leave. As he reached the door, the director called out, 'And tell the Navy we would be very grateful if they got the right aircraft this time. We do not want another *Vincennes* got it?'

The door closed without a sound.

USS Nimitz, CVN 68, Position: Latitude 16N, Longitude 64E

The carrier and its escort group had been steaming at maximum speed for 36 hours, course 350 degrees, to reach this point in the southern part of the Arabian Sea, and without any clear idea why. All they had was the original signal, which ordered them to a position on the 22nd parallel, 360 miles, or about 10 hours, further north, with the rather vague requirement that they were there to stop a rogue civilian airliner that may try and move out of the Gulf to the east within the next few days.

Details on aircraft type had eventually been received, along with what was known about the anti-radar suite it was apparently fitted with. The captain and the air wing commander had signalled for more information on this last twice, but nothing useful had arrived. The air Commander did not like the idea of false radar positions. How the hell were his F14s supposed to find and maybe fire on a target which wasn't where the return said it was?

The captain was less pessimistic. The primary return would still be there and the ship's radar and that of the accompanying AEGIS cruiser were amongst the most powerful in the world. In his opinion, a bit of black paint wasn't going to fool his ships, no sir! Of course, he knew it all depended on the aircraft coming within range, which is why they were positioning the ship directly under the airway system on the route from Dubai to Bombay.

An ensign from the signal office knocked and entered. 'Signal from stateside, sir' The young officer handed it over.

The captain read it and looked up. 'Okay, gentlemen, it looks as though this has just got serious. This aircraft left Bahrain about 90 minutes ago, apparently, destination down as Bombay, ETA closest point to us in about 45 minutes. Last reported position is SULAR, where the airway its on, Romeo 219, crosses airway Golf 787. At the moment it is still under radar from Muscat, but that drops out at a position called MAROB. After that, its procedural to position SUMOS, where Bombay radar will pick them up. So, looking at the plot, we have about 400 miles of empty in which to get this fixed. Naturally, it is not expected to arrive at SUMOS. The info here is that a turn north up the Pakistan/Iranian border area is likely, probable destination red land somewhere. They say that endurance on the figures to hand is about 5 hours max, so that narrows it down a bit, although it is an SP, and if memory serves it could be capable of much more than that.'

Pointing at the ensign, he barked, 'Get those people in Bahrain to double-check the fuel loading record over the last couple of days, now!' Turning to his air wing commander, he said, 'I've got a bad feeling about this. From the signal, this thing is calling itself Trans-pac 102, but I don't think that will help much. Get a couple of your boys up there. We will move the airborne radar piquet further east and just north of the airway, then position the F14s so they are between it and the Pakistani coast. Put another radar piquet to the south and have a couple more F14s at readiness. What are you hanging on them?'

'I've loaded them with two Phoenix each, plus the usual AIM9Ms.'

'Yeah, I guess that will do. I am concerned by the point you made earlier about target acquisition. Now that it is going to be out of range of the ship's radar; it could get down to the AIM9s, or even guns, if this stuff they are supposed to have is as good as they say. Certainly, the Phoenix will have trouble if it is. It's a good job the damn thing is wired; at least we will know where it really was and that will give us a track to work on.'

On the flight deck the launch process was under way, the course now 300 into the prevailing wind, to help the aircraft into the air. The first to go, as always, were the Lockheed S3 Viking tankers. *Nimitz* had two on board and both were at the start of the launch sequence, and as usual they would also be the last to return. These were followed off the waist catapult by the first of the Northrop Grumman E2 radar aircraft, then by a pair of heavily-laden F14s from the two bow cats. As the last aircraft disappeared into the night. Two more similarly laden F14s were positioned on the forward catapults with the second E2 at the waist.

Langley, Director's Office

The aide stood at the door, 'Sir, I have to report that satellite surveillance of the target aircraft has been lost. In fact, it appears that while we have them up to the point of landing in Bahrain, at some stage after that the system has gone off-line. We have been on to the Brits about it but as of now they are saying that it is a foolproof system and the only way it could go off-air is for it to be switched off or destroyed.'

'Have the navy picked it up yet?'

'No, sir, not as yet. Last reported position was with Muscat centre at a position called SULAR on the airway to Bombay. At this stage it looks as though they are doing exactly what they are planned to do. As suggested, *Nimitz* is concentrating the screen to the north of the airway.'

Once again the telephone interrupted them. The director listened, reached across and turned up the speaker. 'This is a satellite recording of a radio transmission from Air Traffic Control at Muscat a few minutes ago.'

"Trans-Pac 102, Muscat centre? 102, go ahead. Trans-Pac 102, we appear to have lost your transponder. Roger, 102, we will try the other unit." A brief pause, then, "Trans-Pac 102, still no return, confirm operations normal. Primary return shows you well north of the airway and dropping out of radar coverage." There is another pause, then a series of calls from the ATC centre at Muscat. From Trans-Pac 102, there is nothing – it had disappeared.

Trans-Pac 102

The two large screens of the defence system were blank as Shaun got up and moved to the small upper deck galley on the left side of the cabin. He was about halfway into fixing up three trays for a long overdue meal when the automatic oral warning called him back to the console. Glancing at the screens, he could see nothing, but the steady amber light indicated that a hostile radar sweep had been sensed. The data that followed indicated a surface transmitter at a range of about 300 miles. He slid into the seat and put the headset on. 'Jim, we just had a single pass from a surface radar at a range of around 300 miles, from a position to the south east of us. It's got to be a ship, and for us to pick it up at that range it has got to be something big. Didn't Pete mention the Yanks were getting involved in this? My guess would be one of their carriers, which is not good news. What do you think about coming right, onto a heading of say 240? It would keep us at about this range from it, whatever it is.'

'Okay, but don't forget the radar at Mesirah; it will put us pretty close to that, won't it?'

'Looking at the plot, we will be 200 miles at the closest point, and if this stuff works as it should, we will slip by, I reckon. Anyway, I think we have a better chance with that than mixing it with the US Navy.'

'Okay, 240 it is,' Jim leaned forward and wound the new heading into the course selection indicator and the SP slowly turned onto the new heading.

Shaun was just about to return to the galley when the threat alert resumed its noisy call, only this time the warning light was red, indicating a serious and imminent danger. A glance at the screen confirmed that airborne radar, at a range of 150 miles to their east, had illuminated them. The automatic system that corrupted their position was active and the interrogating radar would receive a position some 50 miles to the north of their actual position.

As he watched the screen, the individual return became three, two of which detached and accelerating, moved towards the position of the false return at high speed, indicating fighter aircraft. Shaun supposed F14s or F18s. Each aircraft was sweeping with its attack radar, the on-board unit was using the continual sweeps from the fighters to update the plot on the hostiles.

'We've got another problem, fellas. Looks like radar equipped aircraft, two of which are fighters in our 8 o'clock, 150 miles out; the two fighters are closing fast, altitude is about what we are. They are currently heading for the corrupted position to the north of us. Any ideas?'

As he spoke, Shaun watched the number 2 aircraft turn through 180 degrees and head back. However, the lead continued to the false position, slowing as it did so. Shaun relayed this to the other two, then, and voice getting a little tense, he said 'The lead is turning towards us, looks like he may have picked something up, he's still at about our speed, though.'

Within seconds, there was a large flash in the sky some 5 miles ahead of them and off to the north.

Jim, temporarily dazzled by the flash, recovered quickly, calling over the interphone, 'Christ! The bastards are shooting at us. I'm going down to the deck, fellas. The descent at idle will reduce the heat signature and also make the radar range less once we get down there. Okay?'

'With you, Jim, let's go,'

Jim disconnected the auto pilot, slamming the thrust levers back to idle, he rolled on 40 degrees of bank and pushed the SP into a dive for its life. Raising the airbrakes, he allowed the speed to build up to the maximum allowed and at Mach .92, the aircraft descended at 9,000 ft per minute. The noise level increased rapidly, making speech between Jim and the Digger impossible outside the interphone circuit. The Digger had anticipated the dive and already had the cabin descending.

CVN 68 Nimitz

The radar plot had shown only the string of aircraft on the airway. All were identified from their transponder codes. There was no sign of Trans-Pac 102. However, there was a noticeable gap in the stream of aircraft where it should have been, and it was here that the ship's radar was concentrating; here, and the area to the north of the airway. At this range the operator was not optimistic and until the radar E2 Hawkeye's system came online, he did not expect to see anything. The northern piquet called in, the aircraft's radar picture was downloaded to the ship's system, giving coverage well beyond the surface unit's ability, but again there was no sign. Then, just as the ship resumed its northerly course, a single blip, a weak primary return, appeared in the lower left hand side of the large screen. Just one blip, then nothing. However, it was enough to alert the operator who called the second Hawkeye, just launched, and presently climbing out on a heading of 270 to cover the area to the south of the airway. Critically, this aircraft was operating alone. The nearest fighters were with the first E2 some 400 miles to the north.

'Nightjar 15, Ragtime.' Ragtime was today's call sign for the ship and Nightjar 15 the recently launched E2.

'Go ahead, Ragtime.'

'Nightjar 15, possible contact bearing 250, range 280 miles primary return only, no longer illuminating.'

'Roger, Ragtime, Nightjar is going active.'

The operator on the second E2 turned on the radar system and almost immediately picked up a weak return on the bearing and range given. However, after just two sweeps the target disappeared, only to reappear at a position some 50 miles further north. The radar operator, who was unaware of the significance of the apparent shift, put it down to an anomaly in the aging equipment. He in turn called the new position of the target to the ship as he programmed the system, allowing the ship instant access to his screens. The ship's system, having been isolated from the airborne unit at the critical time, remained unaware of the shift.

'Nightjar 15, I'm pulling Victor 1 and 2 off the northern screen and sending them down to investigate. Take up a heading of 255 and follow. Estimated speed of the target is Mach .86, so he is going to lose you. Looks like it might be our baby. Victors should be with you in 10 minutes or so. Victor 1, acknowledge.'

The F14s on the northern screen acknowledged and turned south to close on the second Hawkeye, going to full afterburner as they did so.

As a precaution, the tactical controller called for the launch of the next two F14s to replace the northern patrol and the positioning of a further pair to instant readiness on the catapult. He estimated that the two presently closing on Nightjar 15 had about 45 minutes fuel, so he called one of the S3 tankers, also wrong-footed to the north, to follow them south. With everything he could think of done, he sat back to watch the action.

The F14s closed on the radar aircraft and, having downloaded the target data to their own attack radars, continued on towards the position of the target. The instruction was to intercept and escort it to Muscat, but they did not have sufficient fuel for that.

'Ragtime, Victor 1, we have 30 minutes remaining, so escort to Muscat is not an option. Advise.'

'Ragtime, Roger, we are about to launch back-up and the tanker is due north, range 200 miles. Victor 2, break off and top up. Victor 1, continue with the target.'

The second F14 broke off, turning north, leaving Victor 1 to track the target alone.

The range decreased rapidly; soon both the pilot and the radar operator were looking in the expected position. Neither saw anything.

Closing to easy visual range, even at night, the pilot called in, 'Ragtime, we should be right alongside this thing now and there's nothing.'

'Confirm, no sign of anything?'

'That's it, Ragtime, zip.'

'Nightjar 15, Ragtime, we show nothing other than the target at that position. You got anything like a weak primary north or south of it?'

It was then the operator remembered the initial return. 'Nightjar 15, we show nothing now, but right at the start of this we got a couple of position readings off to the south, about 50 miles, but then the current return showed.'

'Damn it, Nightjar, you should have told us. Victor 1, turn onto 180 and see if anything comes up. Ignore the target return, it's false. Acknowledge.'

'Victor 1, roger.'

The F14, now getting very short of fuel, stayed subsonic and turned south. After 10 minutes, the radar operator picked up a faint trace at 50 miles, with the same altitude speed of about 500 knots or Mach .86.

Calling it in, the trace came and went on his screen. The Phoenix missiles' target acquisition radar would not lock on.

'Ragtime, Victor 1, we have a weak target at 50 miles. Missile lock is not possible, will close for a visual. We are down to 10 minutes of motion lotion, advise?'

The Commander Air moved into the corner of the control room with the Captain. A call was made to the Pentagon, already on an open line. The instruction was there in a minute. 'Destroy it.'

'Victor 1, Ragtime, you are clear to launch, use Phoenix if you get a lock on, AIM9s if you can close the range.'

'Roger, Victor 1.'

On board the lone F14, the radar operator tried desperately to hold the target long enough for the missile system to lock on, finally calling to the pilot, 'Okay, that's it, Fox 1.'

Under the port wing, the long ugly missile dropped away. As the motor lit up with a flash, it disappeared into the night. The operator watched it track the target and at the point when the on-board systems would normally take over to home on the target, the target disappeared again, leaving the missile blind. It continued on its original heading, the on board radar system frantically trying to re-acquire the rogue aircraft. Eventually, at the limit of its range, it self-destructed.

The pilot, who had watched it all, could only manage, 'Shit! That was expensive.'

Down to its last few minutes of fuel, they picked a faint infrared trace at about 20 miles. More in desperation than anything else, they launched the two AIM9 missiles.

It was at that point that the SP began its rapid descent and with the engines at idle and all but invisible in infrared, the missiles soon lost any chance of homing on the target. Each followed the last known track until fuel was expended and again the self destructs destroyed them. The F14, with trouble of its own, had already turned, in response to the vectors received from the radar aircraft, to rendezvous with the tanker. It was going to be touch-and-go.

Within 2 minutes Victor 2, now heavy with fuel and at full afterburner, returned to the chase but it was too late, the SP had once again disappeared. Two more F14s arrived and proceeded to sweep the area out to the limit of their range but of the airliner there was no sign.

Aboard *Nimitz* the captain was endeavouring to explain to the Pentagon what had happened. He was not having a good time.

CHAPTER FIFTEEN

Trans-Pac 102

Jim had levelled off at 1,000 ft above the ocean, using the radar altimeter to do so. Still doing the maximum speed allowed, of 390 knots, the air brakes had been retracted at the bottom of the dive and the four great engines were positively roaring to maintain the speed.

Shaun, who had watched the screens until the chase aircraft eventually gave up, came forward. 'You jammy bastard,' he began as he saw the fun Jim was having low-flying at night. 'I've always wanted to do that.'

Jim, sitting relaxed at the controls, managed a big grin. 'Bloody great fun! Go on, have a go.'

Shaun slid into the right-hand seat and strapped in. 'Handing over.'

'Okay, taking over.' Shaun then spent about 10 minutes flying the huge aeroplane at high speed at low-level, then plugged in the autopilot so they could discuss the next move.

First thing was to climb back up to a normal altitude for, much as this was fun, it was chewing through the gas at an alarming rate. The Digger reduced the thrust, letting the speed bleed back to 290 knots and Shaun selected 34,000 ft and programmed the aircraft to climb.

Turning to Jim, he said, 'Think we should just check the screens as we go up, mate, just in case. I don't know much about naval aircraft, you know range and all, but I reckon we should just make sure they haven't followed us.'

'Sure, I'll do it. About time I had a go with this stuff.' With that he slipped out of the seat and moved into the rear cabin. After a few minutes he gave the all-clear.

It took them about 20 minutes to return to the cruise altitude and the Digger calculated that the whole exercise had cost them about 7 tonnes of fuel or something like 40 minutes endurance at normal cruise.

The actual distance they had to cover was roughly 6,000 nautical miles, which gave a still air flight time of about just over 12 hours, but there were headwinds forecast for most of the flight. They had worked on a ground speed of 450 knots. The flight time would be more like thirteen hours and 30 minutes. With a maximum endurance of 15 hours, they had been quite comfortable, but the loss of this fuel now meant that things could get a bit tight, especially if the winds were stronger than forecast, and forecasting anything over Africa was largely guesswork. It meant they did not have much to play with if anybody else decided to get nasty.

As they approached the African coast at a point about halfway between the French base at Djibouti and the Somali capital of Mogadishu, they were relying on the invisibility of the aircraft to get them through.

Jim, having finished the business of feeding them that Shaun had started what seemed an age ago, sat watching the screens as the aircraft crossed the coast. So far there were no other aircraft to be seen, nor any ground interrogation. In fact, there was not even radio traffic, for as they moved through the airspace, they routinely checked the Jeppesen airways charts for the appropriate frequency for that area and dialled it up and listened. Shaun moved the aircraft a little further to the south to give Addis Ababa a wide berth. The Ethiopians were known to be a little touchy about their airspace. He listened to a couple of aircraft receiving vectors for an approach, but other than that all was quiet.

With Addis Ababa slipping behind, he turned onto a north-westerly heading, through the great emptiness of southern Sudan. Below in the darkness, the mountains slowly gave way to the desert, which would be with them for the next 6 hours.

'So the goddamn navy have screwed up again, eh? Bastards either shoot the wrong thing down or miss the right thing! How the hell can you miss something that big?'

'Sir, the navy is saying had we given them more information on the thing's capabilities, they could have got it. They are also saying it was our idea to put the screen to the north of the airway and that if we had levelled with them they would have covered the south right from the start.'

The look of uncontrolled venom this drew from the director was sufficient to shut down the aide who had been detailed to break the news. 'When I want your opinion, whatever your name is, I will ask for it. Now get out!'

He had just reached the door when the director yelled again. 'And what are the bloody Brits doing about all this? Do they know where the thing is going?'

The young man turned, swallowing hard. 'Er, no, sir, they have no idea. They have found out that it was the original crew who are flying it and they are talking to the Australians to see if they have any idea on a destination. They reckon these guys have had this planned for some time. The Aussies are debriefing their special forces people as we speak, but they haven't come up with anything yet.' Taking a deep breath, he continued. 'The Brits have also have just told us that they appear to have lost the girl who was on the inside. She seems to have disappeared. They are not sure whether Gulf Arab have removed her, or she has jumped ship on her own. They seem to think it's the latter. Their man there is saying that she now seems to have developed a connection with a group of Omanis we were unaware of. They can't say what it's all about, but this group do not seem hostile. Quite the reverse, in fact. Trouble is, they also seem to have their own agenda and the information the Brits are getting is that these people, the girl and the flight crew were all seen together on one occasion.'

'Holy cow, man, how the hell is it that we are the last to know about all this? Here we have a bunch of time-expired aviators, a girl and a bunch of locals running fucking rings around us, and I'm including the bloody Brits in the 'us'. What the hell do we know about these people? Has anybody checked their backgrounds? Up to now they've made complete arseholes of us. Get me all we know and get me Sir Robert on the phone.'

MI6

Sir Robert replaced the handset. The call had not been pleasant. The fact that the 'cousins' had failed to intercept the aircraft was some conciliation, but at the end of the day it was undeniable that his own department had performed badly. Not only had the aircraft been able to leave without their knowledge, it had been two hours before they had found out that it had gone at all. Now they had lost the girl as well and there was this new group of Omanis that had appeared from nowhere, about which they new nothing. Nor, it seemed, did the Bahrain police.

He had immediately queried the range of the aircraft and been told that according to the fuel uplift from Bahrain it was in the order of 5 hours. At an estimated 500 knots, it gave the eastern states of central Africa as the achievable destination, at least on the last heading the aircraft was known to be on, allowing that it had spent quite a long time going in what appeared to be the wrong direction.

He stood looking at the map of the target area. It was a fact that, unlike the old days, there were very few states there that the West could rely on. Far from it. Almost all, with the possible exception of Kenya, could be considered hostile, with Sudan top of the list. The range scale he had on the map gave Beira in Mozambique as the southern limit, out across the continent and round to Cyprus in the north. His bet was

Sudan, with Khartoum top of the list. All very well of course, but neither MI6 or the CIA were exactly flavour of the month here. Information was going to be hard to get. He had given up the idea of finding the thing before it landed.

Sensing that there was likely to be political fallout from this mess, he had already established that the blame rested entirely with the department responsible for overseeing these developments. Somehow, he did not see Victoria's career proceeding much further after this. He had also put in place a notice that the crew were to be considered hostile and dealt with accordingly. Ironic really, as he had been quite willing to accept, and even encourage, their elimination from the beginning. That was business, though; this was now personal, for it was them he blamed, more than anyone else, for the current situation. Even if they survived, he would see to it they never worked again.

There remained one area that he could take action and, given his frustration everywhere else, he would enjoy this.

Leaning forward, he picked up the phone. 'Get me the Jordanian Consulate on the phone. I want to speak to Saddim al Hassid, the Cultural Secretary.' He waited while the connection was made, getting the story straight.

'Ah, Sir Robert,' purred the voice on the line, 'so long since we have spoken. Tell me what can the Jordanian people do for Her Majesty's Government?'

'More a question of us helping you out, actually, Saddim.'

By the time he replaced the receiver, he had, along with an entirely sustainable piece of information on a group of dissidents active in Amman, let it be known that, at this very moment, the Iraqi government was being swindled by the very people they were entertaining. No details other than the vaguest suggestion had been made, but he was reasonably sure that Mr bloody Meldrum and his men were in for a difficult time; small compensation for the loss of 15 million dollars, but he felt better. It was always handy to know who worked for who in this game, and for some time British intelligence had been aware of Hassid's pro-Iraqi sympathies.

He was about to leave when his secretary called, advising that the head of Middle East desk was outside seeking a few minutes.

He groaned. 'What now? Oh, send him in.' From the man's body language, he knew he was in for more bad news.

'I am afraid there have been a couple of developments, Sir Robert.' He paused, but his chief said nothing. 'Er, the last cargo of guidance systems have stopped moving, according to the satellite. In fact, they have been static for about two hours now and we and the Americans feel that this is the final destination. It's a position right up against the Jordanian border in the desert. They have told the Israelis and I think we can expect a call any time. They will want to go in and eliminate the threat, as you know.'

'Damn. And the second thing? You said a couple.'

The head of the Middle East desk looked even more uncomfortable. 'It seems we may have badly underestimated the range of the aircraft, sir. From what we can make out the aircraft was full of fuel when it left, not the 60 tonnes we thought.'

'What?' Sir Robert exploded. 'How the hell could your people have missed that?'

'Well, sir, it's apparent that the crew have been planning this for some time. We had to go back as far as the transit of Muscat to pick this up. What they did was fill it up there and from then on they just topped it up. Of course, until we got the figures from Muscat we only saw them replacing what was used on the previous leg and this did not raise any suspicion.'

'Yes, and what does it mean in actual terms? How bloody far can it go?'

'Well, as near as we can tell, they have over 15 hours endurance, which means just about anywhere in Africa, or they could even turn around and have another go at the north, assuming that this was their original intention, of course. It also means anywhere in Europe, not that we see that as likely, then there is Australia. They could make the north west of Western Australia, we think.'

'You think?' he roared. 'Christ, I don't think any of you have thought at all. What this means is that these three men have made complete fools of the lot of you. You haven't got a bloody clue where they are, where there going, or what they intend. In fact, you know nothing, do you?'

The head of the Middle East desk remained silent. There was no point in doing anything else when the chief was in this sort of mood. He did note that Sir Robert had been careful not to include himself in the blame stakes. Realising that heads were going to roll however this turned out, he resolved to do a bit of butt covering of his own.

'And what about this Fitzgerald character, what have we got on him?'

The man shuffled on his feet in some discomfort. 'Er, I am afraid that isn't the best of news either sir. It appears he was involved in a couple of our more delicate operations in the 60s. He's ex-military, of course, and our estimation is that he is quite capable of something like this. He was being looked at as a potential field worker for us but he left in the early 70s under a bit of a cloud. Something about shooting his CO in the backside. It appears Fitzgerald and the man's wife were having a thing and his boss found out about it. Word is the boss was a bastard anyway; knocked the women around, that sort of thing.

'After he left the service, he seems to have done some time in Vietnam, which may have been where he teamed up with the two Australians. Canberra has told us that their two were both there, in the military and as civilians later. Thing is that the three of them could quite easily pull something like this off.'

'Could? What do you mean, could? These bloody people are running rings around us.'

The telephone flashed and he was dismissed with an impatient wave. 'Saul, been expecting your call. Can I suggest a conference call with the director in Langley? Save us a lot of time, don't you think?'

This was agreed and within minutes the three of them set in motion the most hostile act one nation could commit on another.

As the arrangements were completed, the staff in the Israeli embassy were already on the lines to Tel Aviv. The process of surgically removing the latest threat to their homeland was on the move.

The raid was planned and approved for tomorrow night with the KC135 tankers getting airborne at around 2300 local Tel Aviv time, 2000 GMT. These would be followed by pairs of F15Es, the two-seat fighter-bomber version of what was still the most useful aircraft in the western world. These would be armed with stand-off smart bombs and laser designator pods. They would top-up from the tankers and then, on a predetermined sequence, such that the strikes would, as near as possible, all be made at the same time. They would head east at high speed, across the southern most part of Jordan, before turning to their specific targets. They were to be accompanied to a point 150 miles inside Iraq by the Israeli Air Force's Wild Weasel F4 Phantoms. Their job was to jam both Jordanian and Iraqi radar. The F4s were, in turn, to be escorted by relays of F16s armed with HARM anti-radiation missiles to protect them from any SAM missile threat, and the usual AIM9s, in the unlikely event that the Iraqi fighters wanted to have a go.

Trans-Pac 102

As they left Khartoum behind them, having passed it some 200 miles to the south, they finally relaxed. There had been nothing on the screens or on the radio for nearly two hours now. Sitting there through the long night, they each realised just how tired they were.

Eventually Shaun, now at the controls and sipping yet another cup of coffee, said to the other two, 'You guys get some shut-eye. We've programmed the INS to join airway G660. All's quiet and going to stay that way for a couple of hours at least, I reckon. I can handle things for a while.'

Neither of them said a thing. Each slid down in the seat and was asleep within seconds.

The plan was to listen on the en route frequencies as they approached the southernmost of the trans-Sahara airways, G660; they were going to try and pick up the call sign of a flight that was at least an hour and one flight information region behind them. They would then adopt this call sign and use its clearances if it became necessary to identify themselves on the way across Africa. This would only happen if the aircraft was detected and this seemed unlikely. Of course, the legitimate aircraft following was going to have all sorts of problems with ATC if they did this, as his slot would have already been taken, but by then they would be on to the next control. As it was, it would only work in Africa where the point-to-point communication between each country's ATC was so poor it relied on the actual aircraft to make its position known. This and the fact that the airway they intended joining was little used at this time of year, being mainly a Hadj pilgrimage to Mecca route, meant that they would probably slip through before anybody realised what had happened.

CHAPTER SIXTEEN

Miami

Mike O'Hara had known Jim and the Digger since the days of the Vietnam war. He had been flying F4s in the USAF on ground attack then. Jim, on the other hand, having left the Australian Air Force some time before, had the much more sedate job of flying between Bangkok and Saigon on one of the many R and R troop contracts. Mike had, on the occasion of their first meeting, come to the end of yet another monumental binge session and having missed his scheduled flight, asked Jim for the jump seat back to Tan Son Knut, Saigon's airport.

From there a firm friendship had grown, such that in the ensuing years each had helped the other out on a number of occasions. Having left the air force soon after the end of the war, Mike had tried the airline world and found it too tame after his previous life. Eventually he had settled for a while with Southern Air Transport out of Miami, flying C-130 Hercules.

Southern was just about the worst kept secret of the time. There were very few who did not know that it was heavily funded by the CIA. Its primary role in life was to resupply those forces in the world seen as being in opposition to governments the good old USA did not like. As a result, he had spent a lot of time in South Africa and Angola. It was here that their paths had crossed again.

It had been in Johannesburg that Jim had introduced him to Shaun. At that time, the three of them were operating for a company that was heavily involved in Mozambique, a country then flirting with the Russians. It was the cause of considerable mirth that they realised they were working for opposite sides.

Nobody gave a damn, though, as at this stage in their lives they realised that all politicians were corrupt bastards – the only difference was the degree.

As the political scene changed, Southern was not needed and was soon reduced in size and interest. Mike had moved on. Not far, though; in fact, just across the airfield at Miami, where he started a small charter business. It had been one of the few success stories in an industry littered with failures and he was now a wealthy man. He still kept his hand in and particularly looked for the odd job for himself, leaving the mundane business of making more money to his small staff of pilots.

Jim's call a few days ago had been like a breath of fresh air. He had been moping around the office, bored out of his skull until then. Now the game was on again, he could feel it. Something big was going down – he just knew it. His old mate Jim would not call in such a mysterious way for nothing. His pilots, long used to his moods and careful to avoid him when he was bored, smiled and relaxed. The boss was happy again and they were glad of it because, tough on them as he was, they knew he would always defend them in a dispute. He was a good man to have on your side.

He had been asked if he could position a Gulfstream IV aircraft to Sal Island at short notice. Also, if the discreet disposal of a 747 was possible, the potential buyer had been identified, but contact through a reliable intermediary would be required. There was an added requirement for some temporary hangar space capable of taking the aircraft in Sal whilst the negotiations took place.

As it was, he knew the place quite well. It was an airfield that occupied most of an island in the Cape Verde group off the coast of West Africa. It had been paid for by the old government of South Africa and was used as a refuelling stop on the run to Europe, when the transcontinental routes had been closed to them. At that time, the Cape Verde Islands, like

Angola and Mozambique, were a Portuguese colony and the provision of a large airport, of international standard, free, was something Lisbon jumped at.

Inevitably, its use for this purpose was very short, for as the Portuguese government withdrew from its colonial empire, the Cape Verdes, like all the others, felt obliged to do the ritual flirt with communism, swapping one corrupt and destructive regime for another. None of which helped South African Airways, of course, for one of the first things the new order did was to close the airfield to them.

The lifesaver here was Boeing's long-range 747, which removed the need for a stop completely.

Sal had, like so many places, slumbered on with the occasional charter to add to the daily Lisbon service.

That his old friends had chosen this place only added to the interest as far as Mike was concerned, and when the second call had come he was ready to go within the hour.

He had spent the time until then ensuring that the one hangar large enough on the field was available and would remain so. He had also contacted an aircraft broker he knew to be discreet and informed him that his services may be required in a few days.

He had chosen his most senior pilot, ex-air force like himself, to accompany him and he took two more of his most reliable men along as well. Somehow he figured there would be something for all of them in this. Like Mike, Frank Johnston was no stranger to the less salubrious parts of the world and the people that infested them.

The call to move had come from Shaun and the Gulfstream IV was airborne within the hour, heading east across the central Atlantic.

The turn to join the airway G660 had been made without any difficulty, the INS system holding the selected heading of 300 until the programmed air route was captured by the system.

Now, heading more or less due west, they were well out over the desert, crossing the border between Sudan and the Republic of Chad, at a position called GENEINA or GNA as it was shown on the Jeppesen chart.

'Bloody great place for a holiday that would be,' Jim murmured.

Below them, the desert, like the night, continued, seemingly endless.

Jim had taken over about 15 minutes ago and the Digger, stirring, quickly checked over the panel, which until then had looked after itself, but now needed a few adjustments to balance the fuel in the various tanks. That done, he looked forward. 'Tea or coffee, Jim?'

'Tea, thanks, Dig. Wouldn't mind something to chew on as well, if you can find anything back there.'

Digger got out of his seat, stretching as he did so. 'See what I can do.'

Shaun remained slumped in his seat, dead to the world.

The call, when it came, made Jim jump. It had been quiet for so long they had begun to feel they were the only aircraft in the air. 'Khartoum, Saudi 517.' There followed a position report, placing the aircraft at the eastern border of Sudan and westbound. The Saudi crew had even been good enough to give their destination, Dakar in Senegal; ideal as it was just a short hop from there to Sal.

Soon after they passed the Sudan/Chad border, Jim called the Digger. 'Better wake Shaun. Not sure about this place. By rights it should be as hick as the rest, but they had a run-in with Gadaffi in Libya a while back and the French were down here helping out, so it could be a bit more First World than we expect.'

'Okay, mate, I'll get him up.'

Shaun, back on the panel, sat looking at the large radar screen. So far, so good. He figured the dangerous bit would be as they neared the capital. It would be here that any sophisticated systems would be based if they were anywhere. As he watched, the yellow threat light flashed a couple of times, finally settling to a continuous, menacing glow, one level below a full alert. The on-board system had detected an interrogating radar somewhere currently below the level where a return from the aircraft would be seen, so the defensive systems were in passive mode, the aircraft invisible to the primary sweep. A quick discussion took place and it was agreed that on this occasion the corrupting shield would be deactivated and the ground station would be allowed to see the aircraft, but only its primary return. The defence system was switched to its standby mode and within a couple of minutes a call for identification was requested from the ground station at Ndjamena, the capital of Chad.

Jim replied, giving his call sign as that of Saudi 615, 'Jedda to Dacca', with their altitude and the appropriate estimate for the western boundary with Niger. He added that the high frequency radios had been playing up, and that the transponders were unserviceable.

The French controller, well used to this type of operation in these parts, made no comment other than to tell them to call at the boundary at a position called KORUT on this frequency, and then Niamey control in the Republic of Niger on 126.1. He then cleared them direct, thereby saving them about 60 miles, a welcome break as the fuel was still going to be tight.

'Now all we have to do is get there before the real guy gets on frequency. Can you imagine the reception that bloke is going to get?'

'I think we will turn it on for the next one, Jim. That way they will be totally confused, may even put it down to another African situation.'

'Good idea, Shaun.'

MI6

'Any sign of it yet?' Sir Robert glared at the assembled underlings.

The head of Middle East desk, reluctantly elected as spokesman, had to admit there was not. 'No, sir. Since the Americans last position it has not been picked up at all. We have alerted what we have in all the potential funk holes, but with the endurance its got, it's going to be like looking for a needle in a haystack. The Americans are saying they will pick it up on satellite as soon as it gets light. They are already looking to the east, but Africa, especially the west part, is going to be dark for a few hours yet. I think I should point out, sir, that these people have thought of everything so far, and it has to expected that by daylight they will be on the ground and out of sight somewhere.'

'And,' Sir Robert began, 'how the hell do you hide something that big? Bury it? I think not. No, they have an end game here and my guess is that aircraft is part of it. With all that equipment on board, it has got to worth a lot of money. Pity the self-destruct device failed. Any ideas on that? Have the Australians come up with anything? Their Special Forces people been interrogated?'

'Yes, sir. They are saying the transmitter was working when they left the aircraft and that has been confirmed. They do not think their people are involved. Two of their best men, by all accounts.'

'And what about this woman? Any sign of her?'

'Well, that's a bit more promising. We have traced her to a flight to Paris. It appears she told Gulf Arab that she had to return urgently, family trouble. We have her arriving at Paris Charles de Gaulle so far. Feeling is she is headed this way, so we are watching the usual places and her known associates.'

'So you see that as a positive do you? Well, I'll tell you how I see it. You couldn't find her on a pissy little island in the Gulf and now you have lost her in Europe – hardly what I would call progress.'

Trans-Pac 102

They had reached the western edge of the Chad airspace at KORUT, made the call as Saudi 615 to the French controller and been released to the next frequency with Niamey control. However, instead of making it, Shaun activated the anti radar systems and the aircraft was now to all intents and purposes invisible again. Not that they reckoned local radar was going to be a problem as, even if it was serviceable, at this hour of the morning the operator would probably be asleep. Just as they changed to the next frequency they heard the beginnings of a rather puzzled conversation between the real Saudi 615 and a rather tired French radar operator at Ndjamena.

The rest of the run across West Africa was quite peaceful. They called nobody and heard little. There were no queries as to unidentified traffic and all indications were that they were through.

The final part of the flight required them to assume yet another identity and as this was the one they would be arriving with, it had to be more sustainable.

It was the Digger who had come up with the idea. As long ago as the departure from Sydney he had seen a South African Airways SP on the tarmac. What they proposed to do was to assume the registration of this aircraft with the suggestion, if asked, that it had been sold to a private buyer, hence the rather bizarre colour scheme, and that this was the delivery flight. They figured that the aircraft would be long gone before it was realised that there were two of them with the same registration in the world. Chances are this would only occur when the local authorities put the bill into Johannesburg and then only if the SAA accounts people were on the ball and picked it up through their accounting system.

It was quite important that they landed in darkness, however, because the actual aircraft registration painted on the aircraft did not match the fictitious one they were about to assume and the colour was distinctive enough to be remembered. Not only would that lead to awkward questions, as it was still the Australian registration, it could lead the wrong people to them. It was going to a close run thing; already there was a faint light in the eastern sky.

Approaching Dacca from the east, they waited until they were just out of radar range and established on airway UA601. Shaun then switched off all the countermeasures equipment as Jim called Dacca Control, announcing that they were a South African Airways 747 en route from Johannesburg to Sal at flight Level 370, with their position and estimate for the boundary of the Cape Verde Islands control zone. As with the French controller in Ndjamena before him, the man was unperturbed that he had no details, requesting only their registration and clearing them through the airspace of Senegal, politely wishing them a pleasant flight. Soon after they crossed the final boundary it was time for the descent, given by a rather tired, and equally disinterested, Sal control.

Recognising that this was to be the last flight they would have in the aircraft, Jim and Shaun tossed for the final landing. Luck was with Shaun and it was he who occupied the left-hand seat as the roll-out was completed and the tower gave them taxi instructions to the hangar on the west side of the deserted airport. Just before the final shutdown, the tower sleepily reminded them that the captain should report there when he had rested; later today would be fine.

With the light now quite pronounced in the east, they wearily left their seats and descended the stairs to the main deck. The Digger once more disarmed the slide and, rotating the handle, pushed the door open. Mike and his crew had already organised steps and a tractor, so after the briefest of greetings the ground crew had pulled the aircraft into the only large hangar on the field. As the doors were finally closed, the sun burst through the morning haze and bathed the now silent airfield in increasing light. The satellite passing overhead, cameras relaying the images of the coming dawn, saw nothing.

The three men were so tired that long explanations were postponed. Mike's people, who had only been there four hours themselves, took care of securing the aircraft while he drove the three of them to the local guest house, adjacent to the airport. Back at the hangar, the only job required was to paint the new registration on the fuselage and lower wing. This took no more than a couple of hours . The last thing Shaun did before sleep overtook him was to hand Mike the signal that was to be sent to the aircraft broker in New York. These were the instructions as to who it was to be forwarded to. There was a requirement that if the deal offered was acceptable to them, then a crew of three was to be at Geneva airport by midnight, from where they would be taken to the aircraft. Mike glanced at it, nodded and left them.

MI6 that evening

'Well, any news?' Sir Robert barked. He had managed to get about 2 hours sleep in the afternoon and was still feeling groggy. It had occurred to him that he was too old for this business, but given the incompetence surrounding him, he did not feel inclined to delegate. A cock-up here could ruin his career and seriously affect his chances of a peerage, and that would never do.

The heads of the Signals Intelligence branch and the Middle East desk were the two who had disturbed him and he was at once curious. Sigs had not been involved in this so far, but last night he had issued an instruction that the GHQ listening centre at Cheltenham should be instructed to monitor air traffic control frequencies in the African area.

'Well, it's to do with that request we put in for specific monitoring of ATC frequencies in Africa, sir.'

'Yes, have they found it?'

'Well, not exactly, but we think something has happened that may be to do with them. It's bloody clever if it is. We only got on to it by accident.'

He went on to describe how French air force Jaguar fighter-bombers had been scrambled to escort a Saudi aircraft into the capital on the grounds that it did not have a valid clearance. Only after many hours of interrogation and diplomatic activity did the authorities realise that the real question was 'who and where' was the aircraft that had gone through the airspace first, using the Saudi call sign? Belated inquiries with Niamey had drawn a blank, all the aircraft passing through the Niger republic were accounted for.

'We think they may have used the Saudi call sign, knowing they were far enough ahead and realising that the French radar at Ndjamena would be good enough to pick them up. As soon as they got to the border, they appear to have gone silent again. The rest of the place is very unlikely to have anything good enough to cause them any difficulties.'

'And where does this lead us? Correct me if I am wrong, but this aircraft must have landed somewhere about 6 hours ago, in an area that has been in broad daylight for at least that long, so have we heard anything at all? Have the cousins seen anything? After all, they keep telling us they can read bloody newspapers with those damn satellites, surely a 747 is within their capabilities.'

"Fraid not, sir. What we have done is worked out a circle of operational ability for the aircraft. Given its known departure fuel and time in the air we estimate that it must have touched down somewhere in this circle.' As he spoke, he unfolded the map of West Africa, on which a circle had been drawn based on the time and position of the call to Ndjamena.

Sir Robert looked at it with contempt. 'Well, it's only all of West Africa you've got here, and the bloody circle even goes off the map to the west. Couldn't you get one big enough?'

'Yes, sir, we will check that little bit, but we reckon they're on here somewhere. That's the Atlantic out there, only a few islands – not likely.'

'Right! Now we have 3 hours before the game really begins and I want that aircraft found before then. Is that clear? Get those damn military attachés we have spread around the place off their arses and out there, it's got to be found.'

CHAPTER SEVENTEEN

Sal Island, The Guest House

They had slept for about 10 hours and now showered and shaved, each admitted he felt better than he had for days. The fact that the tensions were at last over was much to do with it, and having Mike and the boys here to cover their backs meant that this rest at least was complete. Mike and his people were obviously bursting with curiosity, so having had their first decent meal for two days, the three of them finally relaxed and, gathering in the large old colonial-style lounge, told their story.

One of Mike's great attributes was an ability to let people talk without interruption, and so it was that after an hour or so they had finished. As the story ended it was Frank who broke the silence that followed and all he managed was 'Holy cow!'

'Of course, it doesn't end here.' Jim began. 'The reason we wanted you to get hold of the broker fella is that, as you saw, we have the insurance details on the aircraft. The cover is provided, as near as we can figure, by a company that is either owned or is associated with the new owners of it. We happen to know that the ship alone is covered for $20 million and the special stuff inside is probably worth that again.'

'Hang on, Jim, you aren't proposing to let these terrorist bastards get their hands on this stuff, are you? Hell, I don't think we could go along with that.'

'No, Mike. Come on, you know us better than that. What we have in mind is that your broker mate negotiates the deal with these people for say, $30 mill for the return of their aircraft, $15 million up front in a Swiss account and $15 mill after delivery. Their people need to pick it up from here. We can't go back, obviously, and we reckon the authorities will be searching high and low for it. Here is the best place. Just before they leave, we figured on reactivating the beacon and through that, the destruction facility. That way, your mates in Langley and his mates,' he nodded at Shaun, 'in MI6 will know were it is and they can fix it up whenever they want to, if they want to. Of course, we will tell them it's on the loose again, just in case the dumb bastards miss it. We figure that, with the $3 mill in bullion in the MEC, plus the $15 mill we pick up from the insurance, plus what this little caper has earned anyway, we should all be pretty well set up. We may even get the second $15 mill, but we aren't optimistic. Whatever, there will be plenty to go around. What do you think?'

Mike paused for a few minutes and then burst into laughter and, infectious as it was, the rest of the room followed. Eventually things settled and he said, 'Well, I have got to hand it to you guys, it's a great caper. From where I sit, all the bad guys get shafted and the feds as well. And what's more, I've got some news for you. The broker has already made contact. He was amazed at how quickly they responded to the offer. Of course, they were desperate to know where you and the goods are, but they have agreed to the deal without argument. He asked if we wanted to up the ante a bit as a result. Reckons he has never seen a deal accepted so quickly. I was going to suggest a 20\10 split. That way we get the bigger piece up front. As you say, I think the second payment is a write-off. They aren't going to be too fussed in honouring a deal like this once they have the aircraft back are they? Thing I do find surprising, though, is the speed. I reckon they need this ship tout bloody suite. I reckon they have a job planned for it and losing the aeroplane must have screwed things up big time. It's also got to be something to do with the special gear, otherwise they could easily find another aeroplane. That means they want to go somewhere that is taboo. To me, that says somewhere our side has an interest in, and would probably not allow. Anywhere come to mind?' He continued 'It's my guess it will be Northern Pakistan or Afghanistan. That's the only area that makes sense and with what's been going on there lately, there are bad guys who want to get out, aren't there? So all the more reason to ensure the trace is activated, eh?'

Mike transmitted the revised details to New York, along with the account number in Switzerland to which the deposit was to be made, giving clear instructions with regard to collection, which they all recognised as the point the opposition would try a double cross if they had a mind to. The deal was for a crew of three alone. They were to be positioned to Geneva, from where they would be flown to the aircraft.

They all then made their way back to the airfield where they set about transferring the bullion from the SP to the Gulfstream parked along side. The flight plan to Geneva was for departure at midnight local time and the two pilots that Mike had bought with him were to fly it.

Shaun and Frank were going along to complete the transfer from the aircraft to the bank. The same bank, incidentally, to which, if all went well, the insurance company would be transferring the payout. They would also provide security on the return flight with what was clearly going to be a hostile bunch of guys. With this in mind, Shaun had given Frank one of the Sig handguns Pete Westerman had left behind. The other, he kept for himself; to the two pilots, he gave a Browning automatic each. They reckoned to be back by tomorrow afternoon at the latest, assuming the other lot could get a crew together that quickly. In the meantime Jim, Mike and the Digger would ensure that the locals were taken care of and the SP readied for departure. Then it was just a case of handing the aircraft over and getting out of there.

The run-up to Geneva went surprisingly well. The Gulfstream had taxied into the executive parking area, where it was met by the vehicle from the bank, to which the bullion was transferred.

None of the Swiss occupants of the van or the two car escort were in the least surprised by the cargo. The agent who had accompanied them completed the paperwork with a speed borne of familiarity. Clearly bullion shipments were a familiar event at Geneva airport. Even the security provided was quietly efficient; no fuss, just quiet professionalism. Shaun was impressed.

Using his mobile, Shaun called the broker in New York and was given a local number to call. Calling this number, he gave instructions for the replacement crew to follow. They were to be at the VIP terminal in 20 minutes or the deal was off. Spluttered objections were cut off as he broke the connection. No sense in giving the opposition a chance to get organised. They had agreed.

Shaun and Frank moved over to the small but luxurious building and waited. The other two were completing the final checks for the return flight. Right on the 20 minutes, a taxi pulled up outside and three men in airline uniforms got out.

Shaun approached the Captain. 'Right, Captain, I will not introduce my colleagues or myself. We all know what is going on here. Suffice to say, if you are ready, we will get on the aircraft and take you to the place where you can collect their property. I am sure there will be no trouble, but just so you understand the situation, I should tell you we are all armed, okay? You may make one call to inform your principals that you are on the way.'

The Captain looked at them. 'Actually, sir, you are wrong. We do not know what is going on here at all. In fact, until 6 hours ago, my colleagues and I were on a normal trip. The owner has told us only that we are to do what you say. Once we are in possession of the aircraft you have apparently, er, shall we say, borrowed, we are to fly it to Riyadh and that is it. Perhaps you can tell us exactly what this is all about?'

Shaun thought for a moment. So these three were not part of the inner circle in this. 'Well, Captain, I think it is probably best if you do not get in any deeper. All you need to know is that you should be on your way in 8 hours or so, assuming your people complete the deal, of course. As it is, I think we should get on, so perhaps you gentlemen will follow me?'

He turned and they walked across the tarmac to the Gulfstream.

Apart from an unusual level of military traffic en route to the eastern Mediterranean, the return flight was equally uneventful. In fact, the three crewmen seemed quite ordinary airline people and Shaun found himself hoping they would not get hurt in the fallout from this.

It transpired that their boss a, Sheikh Rashied, who they said ran the airline which was associated with Gulf Arab exports, had agreed a bonus payment for this special job, no questions asked. Once it was done, they were back on the line. It was pretty clear that they had been selected for no other reason than that they were in Geneva on a slip. Realising this, he and Frank relaxed a little.

Arriving back in Sal at midday, the men were none the wiser as to where they were. They were a little surprised at their new steed, the totally black colour scheme of the SP causing considerable comment.

Ushering them into the office they occupied, he found Jim, Mike and the Digger listening intently to the short wave radio Mike had. 'What's going on?'

Jim glanced up. 'Looks as though the balloon's gone up in Iraq. Early story is that the Israeli's have mounted a pre-emptive strike. Got to say it looks like we got out of there in the nick of time. It's almost certainly that stuff we took in that's set this off.'

Shaun glanced at the Gulfstream crew. 'I guess that was what all that extra military traffic was all about on the way back, eh? Okay gents, that's your aircraft. We will show you around her. We have filled her up for you, no charge, tell your boss. Once you're happy you can make the call and once we have confirmation of the payment, I think our business is completed.'

'Just one thing,' the captain began, 'we still have no idea as to where we are, and they are going to ask.'

'Of course. Once the transfer is made, you can make a second call with your location. We are going to be leaving soon after you, so it will be of no consequence then.'

The captain nodded acceptance.

It took no more than an hour to complete the inspection. The only comment made concerned the exotic electronics on the upper deck. The Digger, who was showing them around, avoided detail, saying only that it was special equipment about which they knew nothing, advising them to leave it alone. The captain left the aircraft, stating that he was happy with it.

Shaun handed him the mobile. 'Perhaps you would be kind enough to make the call, then.'

A long series of numbers was followed by a brief conversation in Arabic. 'They are making the transfer now,' was all he said.

'Fine. Well, I think a final cup of coffee and then we check the transfer, and we can all get on our way. Agreed?'

Jim called Geneva about 15 minutes later and it was confirmed that $20 million dollars had been deposited in the account. Smiling, he nodded at the gathered men. 'Okay, boys, that about wraps it up. Captain, you are on Sal Island, in the Cape Verdes group. We have filed a flight plan for you to Riyadh. We have taken the precaution of using the southern route, given all the trouble that seems to be going on up north. I think you will find the fuel we have loaded is sufficient, plus a couple of hours in reserve. Hopefully, you won't need it. Dig, if you would just close the holds for these folks, we will get the tractor hooked up and push you back out.'

As the three Arabs moved to the steps, the Digger climbed up to the hold to shut it, but before doing so he reactivated the beacon. Then, as the door slowly closed, he and the others pulled all the ground equipment away and opened the huge doors of the hangar. One of Mike's men driving the tractor pushed the aircraft slowly back into the open air, while the Digger, now on the headphones at the nose, went through the start sequence with the new flight crew.

Within a few minutes, all four engines were running, the final connection severed and the SP taxied into the darkness. The three of them stood and listened. As the great engines increased to take-off thrust, they watched the lights at the wing tips accelerate down the runway, slowly at first, and then more rapidly to the point were the nose was lifted and she was airborne. All too soon, even the sound had disappeared. Each of them stood alone with their thoughts, the last link with a lifetime now gone, to a very uncertain future.

Mike, sensing the moment, waited. He coughed lightly. 'Better get going, boys. They could be all over this place in a few hours and we want to be well away, I reckon.'

'Ain't that the truth? Come on, fellas, last leg coming up.'

Jim led the other two across to the waiting Gulfstream, itself refuelled and ready. Within twenty minutes it, too, was airborne and turning to pick up its outbound track, in this case 270 degrees, westwards out over the ocean as the early morning light slowly overtook them.

The five-hour flight was soon over and the three of them once again stood on an almost empty tropical airfield saying their farewells. This time it was Mike and his team who were going, back to Miami, another three hours to the north.

'We will be in touch in a few days, Mike, we can discuss what we owe you then. Do you need anything up front? We can arrange a transfer today, if you like.'

'No, a few days is fine, Jim. Wouldn't have missed it for the world. Of course, they are going to be after you three, you know that, don't you? City Hall doesn't like to be made fools of, and you guys have pissed all over quite a few City Halls, I think. I'll make the call re the aircraft when I get back stateside. Don't suppose the dumb bastards have picked the signal up yet. Nice touch, Shaun, delaying the call like that. Those poor devils obviously knew nothing about all this. With a bit of luck, they will be out of it by the time some dickhead politician makes up his mind what to do about it.

The Israeli raids had gone off in textbook fashion. Each of the targets had been destroyed, as was confirmed by the transmitters all ceasing to function. The only casualties were an F15 and its escorting F16 on the homeward leg, which inadvertently had a mid-air collision, and even here the three crew involved managed to eject. They were picked up by the helicopter patrolling the Jordanian border. The Jordanian Air Force had prudently stayed on the ground.

With the coming of the morning, the protests began, Jordan with some justification, Syria with none at all and Iraq with impotent blind fury.

In Baghdad, the total immensity of what had just happened sank in very quickly. The war against the Jewish people had just been set back at least 5, and probably more like 10, years. They realised that their Arab brothers would support their protest with strong words in the UN and elsewhere. They also knew that that was all they would do. America and the Zionists had won again, and somebody had to pay. The fact that the intelligence directorate had, only a few hours ago, received a call from one of their most trusted agents in Amman regarding their guests was in no small way responsible for what followed. The need for instant blind and savage revenge could be easily satisfied.

Meldrum and the other two had heard nothing of any of this, of course. The raid on the site nearest the city had been quick; a couple of explosions in a place where loud bangs were commonplace. Heavily involved in another night of decadence, they had ignored it. So the crash as the bedroom door of his luxurious suite hit the wall woke him with a start.

The colonel, with whom he felt he had established something of a rapport, stood there, a look of undisguised contempt on his face. 'Come with me. Now!'

He turned away, but the two soldiers who had accompanied him strode across to the bed. Savagely beating the other two occupants, they grabbed Meldrum by the arms and dragged him out of the room.

He was taken to the prison used for political interrogations, but there was never any intention to interrogate him. The order had been simple; he was to be destroyed. The manner very specific: the purpose to inflict the maximum pain before death. Any information they had would be gained from other sources and, in truth, the colonel did not believe they had any.

Meldrum, still naked, was thrown into an empty, gloomy room. The only light came from the 60 watt bulb hanging precariously from the ceiling.

Only as his eyes adjusted did he notice the vague figures seemingly elevated above the floor at the far wall. As the door was shut behind him, the shivering began. He was cold and in a state of shock. Even so, his curiosity moved him to the rear wall and, as he looked, the horror of what he saw hit him. The two bodies were hanging, large meat hooks thrust deep into the throats. Naked, each was covered in blood from extensive wounds inflicted before death. The wailing began then, and he lost control of himself, the stink unnoticed. The bodies looking down with sightless eyes were those of his operations director and chief pilot. Somewhere in the last sane part of his brain, he realised that there was no future, nothing.

They came for him within the hour, smiling mercilessly.

'So, you have no doubt renewed your acquaintanceship with your friends? I imagine you would have found the conversation a little one-sided,' laughed the colonel. As he spoke, a long bench and a brazier of hot coals was carried into the room. 'Now, Mr Meldrum, you are, of course, aware of our dear president's reputation? He is, shall we say, not a man who suffers fools gladly, and he sees you, I am afraid, as a fool.

'What you will not know is that he is also a great scholar of the history of Britain, particularly that period in the infidel's history strangely referred to as the Dark Ages. We would see that period as one of clear thinking and decisive action, particularly in circumstances such as this.'

Meldrum, fascinated and confused, managed a whispered, 'I don't understand.'

'No, I don't suppose you do. Tell me, did you ever study the period of the twelfth century in British history and one of the kings of that period in particular, a certain Edward II?'

Somewhere in the back of his mind, the connections were made, from schoolboy history to military studies. The slow realisation of his impending fate confirmed as, at last, he focused on the brazier of hot coals and the long piece of metal lying on it, now glowing red in the gloom.

MI6

The fact that the raids had been a resounding success was a considerable relief to both Washington and London. The line to Langley ran hot as Sir Robert discussed the loose ends with the director. It was being referred to, by their political masters, as a major event in the war against terror.

There remained the question of the rogue aircraft and the crew, together with the odd individual who would have to be sanitised.

The call alerting them to the fact that the aircraft had returned to the Middle East had come too late for them to do anything about it and the aircraft was now safely on the ground in Riyadh. With the power off, the trace was not currently active, not that it mattered in Riyadh, because there were sufficient agents in the place to keep an eye on it. He had made sure it was under a 24 hour watch.

Having disposed of the aircraft's human cargo in such a dramatic way, Sir Robert's thoughts had returned to the original purpose of the purchase of this particular aircraft and it occurred to him that it would be in their interests to see just what it was intended for. Of course, he would have the usual problem with 'the cousins'. They would doubtless want to destroy it as soon as it came alive again, being exasperatingly consistent in these matters. However, as he held the key to the self-destruct codes, he felt they would eventually see his point of view.

Yes, all in all, the peerage was looking quite secure again. As to the crew who had caused them so much trouble, they had disappeared. It also seemed that the half payment in bullion his Bahrain people had managed to acquire seemed to have been a little light as well. He suspected the cause was in that basket, too. No matter, they would turn up eventually and he would deal with them when they did.

The Australians had agreed that the two Special Forces men involved would be quietly retired with threats of dire retribution if anything was said. Fortunately, the Australian SAS had not followed the home-grown example where every wretched trooper felt the need to write a book, something that caused HM government considerable grief. Damn it, didn't these people realise book writing was the province of the upper class, not the lower orders? Can't have the wretched plebs getting above themselves, he thought. Good job the Antipodeans had firm control of it.

The girl would turn up, too, and when she did he felt an extension of the threat of a return to Thailand would be sufficient to control her, although the reports from his agent in Bahrain had said she was quite resourceful and not lacking in courage. He might consider using her again. Fluent Arab speakers did not grow on trees.

He would speak to Victoria, currently in the invidious position of being his main scapegoat in the event of adverse comment from on high. She would be given the chance to redeem herself by bringing the female agent under control, might even suggest a little private tryst while she was vulnerable. Yes, that was indeed something to think about.

The last thing requiring his attention was the issue of this strange cell of Omanis that had surfaced in Bahrain. They could be useful. He would instruct the agent there to approach them with an offer. You can never have too many irons in the fire, after all.

EPILOGUE

The Starlight Club, 0400, Present Day

There was an early light in the sky, not that I really noticed it; more a sensation of a long night coming to an end. I had sat and listened for something like five hours, as near as I could figure. The room was quiet, full of smoke, the table littered with glasses and the now-empty bottles of OK rum.

'So that's it,' Shaun said. 'That's the whole story. Well, almost. There was Meldrum and his mates. I guess you might want to know what happened to them. We didn't find out until weeks later. It wasn't nice. After the Israeli raids, they were all seen as potentially responsible and executed – eventually.'

'Apparently, a few people in Washington and London had their butts kicked and there has been the odd suggestion that certain people are not best pleased with us. Threats of retribution, and all that. It's the one loose end we have to tie up really. That's where you come in. We need you to tell the story and get them off our back.'

'Bloody hell,' was all I could manage. A million questions came to mind, but before I could begin there was the sound of sirens and the darkness was disturbed by the flashing lights of police cars. I looked around, anticipating a reaction, but none of them moved, except to look in expectation at the door.

After a few minutes, the double doors were thrown back with a loud bang and two large policemen, Sikhs by their turbans, took up positions on either side. Appearing between them, a senior officer, a superintendent at least, I thought, stood in the doorway waiting as we all did, for his vision to clear. He glanced slowly round the room and settling on our table, a slow smile spread across the handsome face. Only as he moved towards us did the limp become apparent.

As he came to the table, the man I knew as Shaun stood up and they embraced. 'Good to see you again, father.'

'And you, too, Kassim.'

Suddenly, the thing that had been bugging me for hours fell into place. 'Jesus!' I blurted out. 'Now I know where I've seen you before. You're Charlie 2, aren't you?'

Shaun turned, a little embarrassed, but it was the Indian who spoke.

'Long time since you have heard that call sign, eh, father?' He looked at me. 'We know who you are, too. Even I have met you before, I Corps man.'

Puzzled, I waited.

'You recall a raid on a village on the Mahaicony River in 1964? A young boy was one of the few survivors. He was airlifted out by helicopter and his life was saved.'

'You?' I interrupted. 'I interviewed you. As I recall, you were in a state of severe shock.'

'Yes, I was, and this man,' he put his hand on Shaun's shoulder, 'spent days, weeks, getting me out of it. I owe him everything.'

Shaun, now acutely embarrassed, muttered, 'Steady on, Kassim, that's enough.'

'No, father,' he paused. 'You see, he adopted me, sent me to school, encouraged me to become a policeman. I owe him everything.'

The two large Sikhs on the door were grinning from ear to ear, as much at Shaun's increasing discomfort as at the obvious pleasure their boss was having in telling the story.

'It is important that all this is said at last, and I want you to tell the world of it. You tell them that this man and his friends are very special to us in Guyana and we will look after them.'

I had returned to London the next day. The story took me a quite a few days to put together, with a number of calls to the old farm on the river bank in Guyana to clear up details.

It was serialised over three weeks when it was published and after the first few editions there was increasing pressure from the establishment to stop it. Fortunately, Jerry, the editor, was made of sterner stuff and resisted.

A week before it broke, there had been a rumour of an airliner going down on departure from Quetta, the old hill town in the mountains of Balluchistan, in western Pakistan. It was suggested that leading members of Al Qaeda were on board and a bomb was suspected. Snippets of information said that the authorities had been aware of an impending attempt to get them out in a specially modified secret aircraft and had reacted accordingly. There were no survivors.

The strange thing was that when the wreckage was eventually found high in the mountains, it seemed that a considerable amount of electronics equipment was missing. That, and the fact that the remains of the fuselage were painted in a black rubbery compound was never explained.

Soon after publication, an inquiry was instituted at MI6 and a number of changes were made. Sir Robert got his peerage and something else besides. It was felt that the department had been very lucky to escape as well as it had. The loss of a considerable amount of bullion and the embarrassment of the article required a scapegoat and he found himself quietly retired.

His replacement was something of a surprise to everyone. A relatively young newcomer called Victoria Manning now occupied his office. She had as her unofficial advisor on Middle Eastern affairs a certain Maria Fernandez, although Fernandez was currently on holiday in some obscure place in South America.

The two quiet men had disembarked from the Qantas flight at Heathrow's terminal 4. They had joined the aircraft in Singapore on a transit from Perth. Climbing on to the shuttle bus to take them across to terminal 3, they stood out for what they were. Even the civilian clothes could not disguise the unmistakable stamp of the military. Tanned, fit and striking, the girl at the check-in found herself mesmerised.

'We would like to check in for flight British West Indian 794 to Georgetown, Guyana, please, miss,' the one in front said. 'The name's Westerman.'